PLAYS FOR PERFORMANCE

*A series designed for
contemporary production and study
Edited by
Nicholas Rudall and Bernard Sahlins*

HENRIK IBSEN

Hedda Gabler

In a New Translation by
Nicholas Rudall

Ivan R. Dee
CHICAGO

Library of Congress Cataloging-in-Publication Data:
Ibsen, Henrik, 1828–1906.
[Hedda Gabler. English]
Hedda Gabler / Henrik Ibsen ; in a new translation by Nicholas Rudall.
p.   cm. — (Plays for performance)
ISBN 1-56663-007-X (alk. paper). — ISBN 1-56663-006-1 (alk. paper pbk.)
I Title.   II. Series.
PT8868.A37   1992
839.8'226—dc20   92-32377

INTRODUCTION
by Nicholas Rudall

Hedda Gabler is, by common consent, a seminal play in the development of contemporary drama. A deeply psychological work, it examines the forces which cause people to commit otherwise inexplicable acts. The fact that the protagonist is a woman places the play squarely in the forum of the issues facing the emancipated woman in the nineteenth century. But above all this is an actors' play. Each character is drawn with an astonishing and ambiguous richness. While it is a play firmly set in its time, this richness of human detail makes it endure.

Most translations of *Hedda Gabler* do not speak with an American voice. There is, as we have often noted in this series, a need for American versions of major works which are also *speakable* and unstilted.

The translation is intended for the actor. English, unlike Norwegian, tends to avoid the complications of many subordinate clauses. Thus sentences are frequently short. Often the repetition of a phrase or of a single word will give the sense of thoughts being spoken and indeed the illusion of spontaneous speech. The ellipses and dashes in the lines are an aid to the actor in achieving a spontaneous and nonliterary speech pattern.

3

I have preserved the Norwegian names in the text, but it is perfectly acceptable, perhaps desirable, to call Jørgen "George" throughout.

CHARACTERS

JØRGEN TESMAN, a research fellow in the history of culture

HEDDA GABLER, his wife

MISS JULIANA (JULIE) TESMAN, his aunt

MRS. ELVSTED

JUDGE BRACK

EILERT LØVBORG

BERTE, the housekeeper

Hedda Gabler

ACT 1

A large, substantial, and tastefully furnished drawing room decorated in dark colors. In the back of the room a wide doorway with its curtains drawn, revealing an antechamber decorated in a similar style. On the right we can see part of the front room. A folding door leads to the hall. On the left is a glass door (French window), also with its curtains drawn. Through it can be seen part of the veranda and some trees covered with autumn leaves. In the front of the drawing room is an oval table with a tablecloth on it and chairs around it. On the right, near the wall, a large dark porcelain stove, a tall armchair, a footstool, and two small side tables. Also on the right is a sofa with a small round table in front of it. On the left is another sofa. A piano is up center. On either side of the large door are two stands with terra cotta and majolica ornaments. In the rear room can be seen a sofa, a table, and one or two chairs. Above the sofa hangs a portrait of a handsome elderly man in the uniform of a general. Over the table is a hanging lamp with a glass shade. Many bouquets of flowers are arranged about the drawing room in their vases. Other bouquets are still on the tables. The rooms are thickly carpeted. It is early morning. The sun is shining in through the French windows.

Miss Tesman comes in from the hall. She is wearing a hat and carrying a parasol. She is followed by Berte who is carrying a bouquet wrapped in papers. Miss Tesman is a woman of about sixty-five, pleasant and handsome. She is wearing a simple but well-made grey outfit. Berte, who is middle aged, is plain and rather countrified in her appearance.

MISS TESMAN: *(inside doorway, listens, and whispers)* My goodness—I don't think they're even up yet.

BERTE: That's what I told you, miss. The boat got in so late last night. And then...Heavens! All the stuff she wanted unpacked before she went to bed.

MISS TESMAN: Well, let them sleep. But... *(opening French windows)* good, fresh, morning air...that we can give them when they come down.

BERTE: *(by the table—at a loss—flowers in hand)* Please, miss. I don't see anywhere to put these. I think I'd better put them over here. *(puts flowers on piano)*

MISS TESMAN: Well, well, my dear Berte, so you've got yourself a new mistress now. Lord knows it was hard for me to let you go.

BERTE: *(near tears)* It was hard for me too, miss. What can I say? All those happy years I spent with you and Miss Rina.

MISS TESMAN: We must all take what comes, Berte. That's all there is to it. Jørgen can't do without you, you know. He can't, it's as simple as that. You've looked after him since he was a little boy.

BERTE: Yes, but, miss, I can't stop thinking about Miss Rina. Poor thing—lying there, completely helpless. And that new girl looking after her. She won't know how to take proper care of an invalid. I know she won't.

MISS TESMAN: Yes, she will. I'll teach her. But of course I'll do most of it myself. So don't you worry about my poor sister.

BERTE: Well, there's something else too, miss. I'm very much afraid that I won't please the young mistress.

MISS TESMAN: Oh well, at first there may be a thing or two, but...

BERTE: Because I'm sure she's very particular.

MISS TESMAN: Naturally! General Gabler's daughter. What a life she had when the general was still alive. Do you remember when she went riding with her father? Galloping along in that long black riding outfit. And that feather in her hat.

BERTE: Oh, yes, I remember...very well. But I never dreamed that she and young Mr. Tesman would make a go of it.

MISS TESMAN: No more did I. But while I think of it, it isn't *Mr.* Tesman any more. From now on you must call him Dr. Tesman.

BERTE: Yes, the young mistress did say something about that last night. Right away. As soon as they were inside the door. Is it true then, miss?

MISS TESMAN: It is indeed. They gave him his doctor's degree! Just think of that. Abroad, during the trip, you know. I hadn't heard a word about it until last night down on the pier.

BERTE: Well, he's so clever, he is. He could be anything he wanted. But I never thought he'd turn his hand to curing people.

MISS TESMAN: Oh, he's not that kind of doctor. *(nods significantly)* And, well, I'm not supposed to say, but pretty soon you may have to call him something even grander than doctor.

BERTE: Oh, good heavens, what could that be, miss?

MISS TESMAN: *(smiles)* Wouldn't you like to know! *(moved)* Oh, dear God, if only his father could look up from his grave and see what his son has become.... *(looking around)* Berte! What's all this? Why have you taken the slipcovers off the furniture?

BERTE: She told me to. Doesn't like covers on chairs, she said.

MISS TESMAN: Are they going to make this their living room then?

BERTE: It seemed like it. Mrs. Tesman did the talking. Mr. Tes— Doctor Tesman didn't say anything about it.

(George Tesman enters inner room from right, singing to himself. Carries an empty unstrapped suitcase. He is a youngish-looking man of thirty-three. Blond hair. Beard. Carelessly dressed in comfortable lounging clothes.)

MISS TESMAN: Good morning, good morning, Jørgen.

TESMAN: *(in doorway)* Aunt Julie. Dearest Aunt Julie. You came all the way out here and so early in the morning.

MISS TESMAN: Well, I just had to drop by and see how you were.

TESMAN: And I'm sure you didn't get a full night's sleep.

MISS TESMAN: Oh, that doesn't bother me.

TESMAN: But you got home all right? After meeting us? How?

MISS TESMAN: Of course I did...but thank you. The Judge was good enough to see me home.

TESMAN: We were sorry we couldn't give you a ride in the carriage. But, well, you saw for yourself ...Hedda had all those boxes.

MISS TESMAN: Yes, she did. Quite a collection, really.

BERTE: Should I go and ask Mrs. Tesman if there's anything I could help her with?

TESMAN: No, thank you, Berte, you'd better not. She said she would ring if she wanted anything.

BERTE: *(going off right)* All right then.

TESMAN: One moment.... You could take this with you. *(hands her the suitcase)*

BERTE: I'll put it in the attic. *(exits by hall door)*

TESMAN: Just think, Aunt Julie, that suitcase was stuffed full with my papers. You wouldn't believe the things I found in the libraries. Old documents, notes, papers that no one knew anything about.

MISS TESMAN: Yes, well then, Jørgen, you didn't waste any time on your honeymoon.

TESMAN: No, I didn't. But take your hat off. My goodness! Here, let me help you with the ribbon.

MISS TESMAN: *(as he does so)* Ah, dear God, this is just like the old days—when you were still at home with us.

TESMAN: *(inspecting the hat)* An elegant hat you've got here.

MISS TESMAN: I bought it to please Hedda.

TESMAN: Hedda? What made you...

MISS TESMAN: So she won't be ashamed to be seen going out with me.

TESMAN: *(patting her cheek)* You think of everything, don't you. *(puts hat down on a chair by the table)* Now then—over here, by me, on the sofa... we'll sit and chat for a while until Hedda comes. *(They sit. She places her parasol on the corner of the sofa.)*

MISS TESMAN: *(taking his hands and looking in his eyes)* It's so good to have you back again, Jørgen. Right here next to me. Jochum's little boy.

TESMAN: For me, too, Aunt Julie. To see you again. You have been mother and father to me.

MISS TESMAN: Yes. I know that there will always be a place in your heart for those two old aunts of yours.

TESMAN: But Aunt Rina... how is she? Any better?

MISS TESMAN: Oh, no... we can't expect her to ever get better, poor thing. She lies there day after day, year after year. May the good Lord let me keep her a little while longer. Because I just wouldn't know what to do with myself if she... especially now when I don't have you to look after any more.

TESMAN: *(patting her cheek)* There, there, come now!

MISS TESMAN: *(changing her tone)* But you're a married man now, Jørgen. To think it was you who walked off with Hedda Gabler. The beautiful Hedda Gabler. And with all those infatuated young men she had.

TESMAN: *(hums a little, smiles complacently)* Yes... I

have a suspicion that I have several friends who'd like to change places with me.

MISS TESMAN: And that honeymoon! What was it, five? no, nearly six months!

TESMAN: Yes, but I had my research to do, too, of course. The libraries, all those books to read.

MISS TESMAN: Yes, of course. *(confidentially, lowering her voice)* But now listen, Jørgen, don't you ... don't you have something ... special ... to tell me?

TESMAN: About the trip?

MISS TESMAN: Yes.

TESMAN: No, I can't think of anything—apart from what I wrote in my letters. I got my doctor's degree there—but I told you that yesterday.

MISS TESMAN: Yes, I know, but I mean ... what I'm saying is, don't you have any ... any expectations?

TESMAN: Expectations?

MISS TESMAN: My goodness, Jørgen. This is your old aunt you're talking to.

TESMAN: Well, naturally I have expectations.

MISS TESMAN: Yes.

TESMAN: Well, I do expect, with some confidence, to be made a professor one day soon.

MISS TESMAN: Oh, a professor ... yes.

TESMAN: In fact, I am sure of it. But dear Aunt Julie—you know that as well as I do.

MISS TESMAN: *(with a little laugh)* Of course I do. *(changing the subject)* But we were talking about the trip. It must have cost a fortune.

TESMAN: Well, the fellowship was fairly substantial. It helped a great deal.

MISS TESMAN: But I just don't see how you could make it do for both of you.

TESMAN: No, I suppose that is difficult to understand.

MISS TESMAN: Especially traveling with a lady. That makes it much more expensive, doesn't it?

TESMAN: Yes, of course—a little more. But Hedda simply had to have this trip. She *had* to. There was no saying no to her.

MISS TESMAN: No, no, I dare say you're right. A honeymoon abroad seems to be quite the thing these days. But tell me, what do you think of the house? Have you had a good look round?

TESMAN: Indeed I have. I've been up since dawn.

MISS TESMAN: And...? Well, what do you think of it?

TESMAN: I love it. It's quite, quite wonderful. The only thing is... I don't know what we'll do with two empty rooms... the ones between the back parlor and Hedda's bedroom.

MISS TESMAN: *(with a small laugh)* Oh, my dear Jørgen, you'll know what to do with them... when the time comes.

TESMAN: Yes, of course, you're quite right. As my library grows, hmm?

MISS TESMAN: Yes, quite so. It was your library I was thinking of.

TESMAN: I'm really most happy for Hedda—for her most of all. Before we got married she used to say that this was the only house for her. Secretary Falk's town house was the only one.

MISS TESMAN: And to think it came up for sale as soon as you'd left. You were lucky.

TESMAN: Yes, very. Very lucky.

MISS TESMAN: But it will be expensive, my dear Jørgen. It's so big. Terribly expensive.

TESMAN: *(somewhat crestfallen)* Yes, I suppose so. Yes.

MISS TESMAN: Oh, my Lord, yes.

TESMAN: How much do you think? I mean, roughly, hmm?

MISS TESMAN: Well, you won't know till all the bills come in.

TESMAN: Judge Brack was very helpful. He managed to get us very reasonable terms. At least that's what he wrote to Hedda.

MISS TESMAN: Well, let's not worry about it. I've put down a little deposit for you to cover the carpets and the furniture.

TESMAN: Aunt Julie! You can't! Where could you ...?

MISS TESMAN: I took a mortgage on my pension.

TESMAN: *(getting up)* What? But that is yours! Yours and Aunt Rina's.

MISS TESMAN: I couldn't think of what else to do.

TESMAN: *(in front of her)* But that was so ... so foolish of you. Your pension! It's all the two of you have to live on.

MISS TESMAN: Now calm down, there's a good boy. It's only a formality. That's what Judge Brack said. He was kind enough to arrange the whole thing. Just a formality...those were his very words.

TESMAN: That's all well and good. But I...

MISS TESMAN: You'll have your own salary now. And if we have to put a little money down now, at the beginning...well, it's a pleasure to help out.

TESMAN: Aunt Julie, Aunt Julie, Aunt Julie, when will you stop making sacrifices for me?

MISS TESMAN: (gets up, puts hands on his shoulders) What else do I have? You're my only joy. If I can make life a little easier for you, what else is there? You have no father, no mother to help you. And now we are almost there, Jørgen! It's been very hard, I know, at times. But now, my dear, dear boy, you have reached the end.

TESMAN: Yes, when I think of it, I can't believe how everything has turned out.

MISS TESMAN: And those who were against you—all those who stood in your way—they've just... disappeared. Gone. Lost. They have *lost,* Jørgen. And the one who was the greatest danger to you, where is he? He fell the hardest. He made his bed and he must lie in it...fool that he is.

TESMAN: What have you heard...since I went away? Is there any news about Eilert?

MISS TESMAN: Only that he's supposed to have published a new book.

TESMAN: Eilert Løvborg? When? Just recently now?

MISS TESMAN: That's what I heard. But there can't be much to it. I shouldn't think but when your book comes out...that will be something different. What are you writing about?

TESMAN: The Middle Ages... the cottage industries of the Brabart... in that period.

MISS TESMAN: To be able to write about things like that. I don't know how you do it.

TESMAN: Well, the actual publication may not be for some time yet. I have a good deal of material to put in order.

MISS TESMAN: Yes, you collect and you organize. You do it so well. You're my brother's son, Jørgen.

TESMAN: I'm ready, anxious really, to get started. Especially now, here, in the quiet and comfort of this house.

MISS TESMAN: And best of all, dear boy... you have your Hedda... the wife of your dreams.

TESMAN: Yes, Hedda. My Hedda... that's the most wonderful part of it all. *(looking toward doorway)* I think I hear her coming now.

HEDDA: *(Enters from left inner room. Twenty-nine years old. Noble. Elegant. Pale complexion. Steel grey eyes, expressing cold clear calm. Attractive brown hair. Tasteful, loose-fitting gown.)*

MISS TESMAN: *(going to her)* Good morning, my dear Hedda—it's so good to see you.

HEDDA: *(extending her hand)* Good morning, dear Miss Tesman. Well, you are here early. It is so kind of you to come.

MISS TESMAN: Not at all. *(slightly embarrassed)* And did the bride have a good night's sleep in her new house?

HEDDA: I slept quite adequately, thank you.

TESMAN: Listen to that. Adequately, she says. Hedda! You were sleeping like a log when I got up.

HEDDA: Fortunately. But of course it takes time, Miss Tesman, to get used to new surroundings. *(looking to left)* Oh, look at that, the maid has left the doors wide open. The sunlight is just flooding in.

MISS TESMAN: *(going to doors)* Well, then, we can close them.

HEDDA: No, don't! *(to Tesman)* Would you draw the curtains, my dear. It will give a softer light.

TESMAN: *(by door)* Yes, of course, my dear. There now. *(closes curtains)* You have the shade and the fresh air.

HEDDA: Yes, we really need the fresh air in here. With all these flowers. Well, won't you sit down, Miss Tesman.

MISS TESMAN: Oh, no, thank you. I just wanted to see if everything was all right. *(looking around)* And thank goodness it is. So I'll be on my way. My sister's just lying there waiting for me, poor thing.

TESMAN: Give her my love and tell her I'll come and see her later today.

MISS TESMAN: Of course I will.... But *(reaching in her bag)* I almost forgot.... I have something for you, Jørgen.... Ah, here we are!

TESMAN: What is it, Aunt Julie, hmm?

MISS TESMAN: *(bringing out a flat parcel wrapped in newspaper)* Here you are, my dear. Take a look.

TESMAN: *(opening package)* Well, well, well, you kept

them for me! Aunt Julie! *(kissing her)* Hedda, isn't that sweet now?

HEDDA: *(by the sideboard)* Yes, dear, what is it?

TESMAN: My old slippers. Look... my slippers.

HEDDA: Yes, they were a frequent conversation piece during our trip.

TESMAN: Well, I missed them. *(going to Hedda, smiling)* These are the famous slippers. Look.

HEDDA: *(moving to stove)* I don't care to, thank you.

TESMAN: *(following)* No, no. Aunt Rina embroidered these for me. Ill as she was. They mean a lot to me. Fond memories!

HEDDA: *(at the table)* But not for me.

MISS TESMAN: No, not for Hedda, Jørgen.

TESMAN: But I just thought... well, Hedda's part of the family now, and...

HEDDA: *(interrupting)* We are not going to get on with that new maid, Tesman.

MISS TESMAN: Berte! But why?

TESMAN: Yes, my dear, why do you say that?

HEDDA: Look! Here.... She's left her old hat here on the chair.

TESMAN: *(shocked and dropping the slippers)* But, Hedda!

HEDDA: What if someone were to come in and see it...!

TESMAN: No, no, Hedda. That's Aunt Julie's hat.

HEDDA: Really.

MISS TESMAN: Yes, it is. And one thing it's not is old, Mrs. Tesman.

HEDDA: I hadn't really looked at it very closely, Miss Tesman.

MISS TESMAN: *(tying the ribbons)* As a matter of fact, this is the first time I've worn it. The first.

TESMAN: And it's an elegant hat. Very attractive.

MISS TESMAN: It isn't so special, Jørgen. *(looks around)* And my parasol...? Ah, here it is. *(picks it up)* This is mine, too. *(mutters)* Not Berte's.

TESMAN: New hat. New parasol. *(clicks through teeth)* Tut, tut, tut. What do you think of that, Hedda, hmm?

HEDDA: Very nice.

TESMAN: Yes, very nice, very nice. But before you go, take a good look at Hedda. Isn't she beautiful?

MISS TESMAN: As always, Jørgen. As always. Hedda has always been beautiful. *(she nods and starts out right)*

TESMAN: *(following)* Yes, but now there's a kind of aura about her... a kind of glow. She...she... filled out... blossomed on our honeymoon together.

HEDDA: Stop it! *(crossing room)*

MISS TESMAN: *(stopping)* Filled out.

TESMAN: Of course, you can't really see it when she's wearing that dressing gown. But I, who have the opportunity to...

HEDDA: *(by the doors, impatiently)* You have no opportunity, for anything.

TESMAN: It must have been the mountain air, down in the Tyrol.

HEDDA: *(curtly)* I'm just as I was when I left.

TESMAN: Yes, that's what you say. But I don't think you're right. What do you think, Aunt Julie?

MISS TESMAN: *(gazing at her, hands folded)* She is lovely—lovely—lovely. *(goes to her, takes her face in her hands, bends it down, and kisses her hair)* God bless you and keep you, Hedda Tesman—for Jørgen's sake.

HEDDA: *(gently freeing herself)* There, there. Please now...

MISS TESMAN: *(with quiet feeling)* I won't let a day go by without looking in on the two of you.

TESMAN: Oh, please do, please do, Aunt Julie.

MISS TESMAN: Goodbye. Goodbye.

(She exits by hall door. Tesman accompanies her, leaving the door half open. Tesman is heard thanking her for his slippers and reminding her to greet Aunt Rina. At the same time Hedda moves about the room, raising her arms, clenching her fists in quiet anger. She opens the curtains, stands by the door looking out. Tesman reenters and closes the door behind him.)

TESMAN: *(picking up his slippers)* What are you looking at, Hedda?

HEDDA: *(calm, controlled)* The leaves—they've already turned—yellow and withered.

TESMAN: *(wraps up slippers, puts them on the table)* Yes, well, we're in September already.

HEDDA: *(restless again)* Yes...to think...we're already in...September.

23

TESMAN: Didn't Aunt Julie seem a bit strange to you...hmm? Almost a little...cold? What do you think was bothering her?

HEDDA: I hardly know her. Isn't she always like that?

TESMAN: No, not like she was today.

HEDDA: *(leaving door)* Was she upset about the hat, do you think?

TESMAN: No, I don't think so. Not really. Perhaps just a little at first....

HEDDA: But it wasn't particularly polite, was it? To leave her hat just lying around in our living room. One just doesn't do that.

TESMAN: I can assure you she won't do it again.

HEDDA: Well, I'll make it up to her somehow.

TESMAN: Yes, Hedda, it would be nice if you did that.

HEDDA: When you go to see them later, why don't you ask her to come back this evening?

TESMAN: Yes. Yes, I will. Thank you. And there is one other thing you could do...it would make her very happy....

HEDDA: Yes?

TESMAN: If you could stop calling her Miss Tesman ...call her by her first name. For my sake, Hedda, dear?

HEDDA: No. That I just can't do. I told you this once before. I'll try to call her Aunt. That will have to do.

TESMAN: Well, I suppose that's all right. I was just thinking...now that you're part of the family...

HEDDA: *(with a short laugh as she goes to the doorway)* I don't know about that.

TESMAN: *(short pause)* Is something the matter, hmm? Hedda?

HEDDA: I'm just looking at my old piano. It doesn't really go with the rest of the furniture.

TESMAN: When I get my first paycheck I promise you we'll trade it in for a new one.

HEDDA: No, I don't want to do that. I can't part with it. We can put it in there, in the inner room. And we can get another, a new one for in here. Whenever that's convenient, I mean.

TESMAN: *(slightly taken aback)* Yes, well, of course, we could do that.

HEDDA: *(picking up bouquet from piano)* These flowers weren't here last night.

TESMAN: I expect Aunt Julie brought them for you.

HEDDA: *(examining them)* There's a visiting card. *(takes it out and reads it)* "Will be back later today." Can you guess who it's from?

TESMAN: No. Who? Hmm?

HEDDA: "Mrs. Thea Elvsted."

TESMAN: Oh, really? The...uh...sheriff's wife. Miss Rysing, I think her name was.

HEDDA: Yes, that's right. She was always showing off her hair...I remember. An annoying habit. She was an old flame of yours, wasn't she?

TESMAN: Oh, not for long. And it was long before I met you, Hedda. But, she's here in town, hmm? I wonder why.

HEDDA: It's strange that she'd call on us. I've hardly seen her since we were at school together.

TESMAN: Yes. No, I haven't seen her, either...oh, since God knows when. I don't know how she can stand living out there—I mean, out in the back woods, hmm?

HEDDA: *(thinks a minute, then bursts out)* Wait a minute— isn't it...somewhere near there that he... that Eilert Løvborg lives?

TESMAN: Yes, I think so. Somewhere near there.

(Berte enters)

BERTE: Excuse me, ma'am. She's back again. The lady who brought you the flowers this morning. The ones in your hand, ma'am.

HEDDA: Oh, is she? Well, show her in, please.

(Berte opens the door for Mrs. Elvsted and exits. Mrs. Elvsted is of slight build. Soft, pretty features. Large blue eyes, frightened look. Hair is white/gold. Abundant and wavy. A couple of years younger than Hedda. She wears a dark visiting dress, tasteful, slightly out of style.)

HEDDA: *(walks to her, warmly)* Good morning, my dear Mrs. Elvsted. How lovely to see you again.

MRS. ELVSTED: *(nervous, struggling to control it)* Yes, it's been a long time...since we met.

TESMAN: *(giving his hand)* And, indeed, since *we* met, hmm?

HEDDA: Thank you for the lovely flowers.

MRS. ELVSTED: Oh, don't mention it....I...I was going to come yesterday afternoon. But then I heard that you were still on your way home.

TESMAN: You've just arrived in town, hmm?

MRS. ELVSTED: Yes. Yesterday afternoon. I was about in despair when I found that you weren't at home.

HEDDA: In despair? Why?

TESMAN: My dear Miss Rysing... I mean, Mrs. Elvsted...

HEDDA: There's nothing wrong, I hope.

MRS. ELVSTED: Well, yes, there is. And I couldn't think of anyone else to turn to.

HEDDA: *(putting flowers down)* Come... let's sit down ...here on the sofa.

MRS. ELVSTED: Oh, I couldn't... I'm really too...

HEDDA: Of course you can. Come on.

(she draws Mrs. Elvsted down on the sofa and sits beside her)

TESMAN: Well now, Mrs....uh...what is it, Mrs. Elvsted?

HEDDA: Has something happened? Something at home?

MRS. ELVSTED: Well, yes... and no. It's very difficult. I don't want you to misunderstand.

HEDDA: Well, in that case, just simply say what's on your mind, Mrs. Elvsted.

MRS. ELVSTED: Yes. Yes, of course. Well, the thing is—perhaps you already know. Eilert Løvborg has come back.

HEDDA: Løvborg...

TESMAN: *(overlapping)* Eilert Løvborg. Well, well. He's come back, Hedda.

27

HEDDA: I can hear perfectly well.

MRS. ELVSTED: He's been here a week already. A whole week...in the city. It's not a safe place for him. Especially alone. There are people here who would just use him, given the chance.

HEDDA: But my dear Mrs. Elvsted—why is he a concern of yours?

MRS. ELVSTED: *(glances quickly and anxiously at her)* He was the children's tutor.

HEDDA: Your children?

MRS. ELVSTED: I have none. My husband's.

HEDDA: Your stepchildren.

MRS. ELVSTED: Yes.

TESMAN: *(with some hesitation)* But was he—I don't know quite how to put this—was he responsible enough—I mean in his work habits—to be teaching children?

MRS. ELVSTED: For the past two years his behavior has been beyond reproach.

TESMAN: Well, that's good news, isn't it, Hedda?

HEDDA: I heard.

MRS. ELVSTED: Beyond reproach. I can assure you. Without question. But now...knowing that he's back...in the city. And with so much money in his pockets...I am frightened to death for him.

TESMAN: But why didn't he stay with you and your husband, hmm?

MRS. ELVSTED: After his book came out, he just couldn't stay with us. He was always on edge.

TESMAN: Yes, Aunt Julie was saying that he'd published a new book.

MRS. ELVSTED: Yes, a very big new book. It's a cultural history, I believe... with an analysis of the progress of civilization. It came out about two weeks ago. It's already a success—the sales are good and the response so very favorable.

TESMAN: Is that so? It must be something he had lying around from a few years ago. In better days.

MRS. ELVSTED: No. You mean from his earlier work?

TESMAN: Yes.

MRS. ELVSTED: No. It was written when he was staying with us. During this past year.

TESMAN: Well, now. That's very good news, Hedda, isn't it, hmm?

MRS. ELVSTED: Yes, I just hope things don't change.

HEDDA: Have you seen him since you came to town?

MRS. ELVSTED: No, not yet. It was hard to find his address. But this morning I finally found out where he was living.

HEDDA: *(looks at her closely)* Isn't it rather strange that your husband—hmm? I mean...

MRS. ELVSTED: *(interrupting)* My husband...? What do you mean...?

HEDDA: *(also overlapping)* That your husband sends you into town on such an errand? Not to come and look after his friend himself?

MRS. ELVSTED: No, no, my husband doesn't have

time for things like that. And I had—I had some shopping to do anyway.

HEDDA: *(slight smile)* Of course, I understand.

MRS. ELVSTED: *(getting up; restless)* Mr. Tesman, please, this is very important. Please be kind to Eilert Løvborg if he comes to visit you. And he will. I'm sure of that. You were such good friends in the past. And you both do the same kind of work—so I gather—the same kind of research.

TESMAN: We used to, at any rate.

MRS. ELVSTED: And that's why it's so important— why I ask you to—to keep an eye on him. You will do that, Mr. Tesman, won't you? You promise?

TESMAN: I'll be only too pleased to, Mrs. Rysing.

HEDDA: Elvsted.

TESMAN: I'll do all that I can. I promise. You can count on me.

MRS. ELVSTED: *(pressing his hands)* Thank you. You're very kind. Thank you. Thank you. *(nervously)* You see, my husband is not very fond of him.

HEDDA: You ought to drop him a note, Tesman. He might not come by on his own.

TESMAN: Yes, that sounds like a good idea, Hedda. I'll do that, hmm?

HEDDA: And the sooner the better. You could do it now, I think?

MRS. ELVSTED: *(pleading)* Yes, could you? If you could...

TESMAN: I'll do it right away. Do you have his address, Mrs.... Mrs. Elvsted?

MRS. ELVSTED: Yes. *(takes slip of paper from her bag and gives it to him)* Here it is.

TESMAN: Very good. Well, then, if you'll excuse me—I'll go in. *(looking around)* My slippers. Ah, here they are. *(leaving with parcel)*

HEDDA: Write him a nice, warm, friendly letter, Tesman. A long one.

TESMAN: I will. I will. Don't worry.

MRS. ELVSTED: But please don't mention my name. Don't say that I...

TESMAN: Of course not. That goes without saying, hmm? *(leaves, into inner room)*

HEDDA: *(Going to her. Smiles. Low voice.)* There! We just killed two birds with one stone.

MRS. ELVSTED: What do you mean?

HEDDA: You didn't see that I wanted him out of the room?

MRS. ELVSTED: Yes, to write the letter.

HEDDA: But I also wanted to talk to you alone.

MRS. ELVSTED: *(flustered)* You mean about this... this same thing.

HEDDA: Precisely.

MRS. ELVSTED: *(nervous)* But there's nothing more to say, Mrs. Tesman. There really isn't.

HEDDA: Oh, yes, there is. There's a lot more to say. I can see that. Now come. Sit here. *(makes her sit in an easy chair by the stove and seats herself on ottoman)* We'll have a nice, quiet, confidential talk. Just the two of us.

MRS. ELVSTED: *(anxious, looks at watch)* But my dear Mrs. Tesman—I'm sorry, but I really must be going.

HEDDA: Oh, there's plenty of time. Now then. Tell me about yourself, how things are going at home.

MRS. ELVSTED: That's the last thing I want to talk about.

HEDDA: But you can talk to me. After all, we were at school together.

MRS. ELVSTED: Yes, but you were a year ahead of me. I was terribly afraid of you in those days.

HEDDA: Afraid of me?

MRS. ELVSTED: Terribly. For one thing, you used to pull my hair—whenever we passed on the stairs.

HEDDA: Did I really?

MRS. ELVSTED: Yes, and there was one time when you told me you were going to burn it off.

HEDDA: I was just teasing—we were always teasing.

MRS. ELVSTED: I know, but I was so...so silly in those days. And anyway, we've just drifted so far apart—since then. We've moved in such different circles.

HEDDA: All the more reason to get close again. Listen. At school we were quite good friends, really—we called each other by our first names.

MRS. ELVSTED: No, I don't think we did. I think you're mistaken.

HEDDA: No, I'm sure of it. I remember it quite clearly. And we were friends then and we must be friends now. Just as we were. *(moves ottoman closer)* There now! *(kisses her cheek)* You must call me Hedda.

MRS. ELVSTED: *(pressing and patting her hand)* Oh, you're so kind to me. It's not at all what I'm used to.

HEDDA: It will be just like the old days. And I'll call you Thora.

MRS. ELVSTED: It's Thea, actually.

HEDDA: Oh, yes, of course. That's what I meant.... Thea. *(looks at her)* So you're not used to kindness, Thea, is that it? In your own home?

MRS. ELVSTED: A home! If I had a home.... But I don't. I never had.

HEDDA: *(looking around)* I thought it might be something like this.

MRS. ELVSTED: *(helplessly, looking straight ahead)* Yes—yes—yes.

HEDDA: I'm not sure if I remember correctly—but didn't you go to your husband's—to the Elvsted's as a governess at first?

MRS. ELVSTED: Yes, that was my position. But his wife, his first wife, was already very ill, practically bedridden. So I had to take charge of the whole house—everything.

HEDDA: And in the end—afterwards—you became his wife.

MRS. ELVSTED: *(dully)* Yes. I did.

HEDDA: Let's see, how long ago was that?

MRS. ELVSTED: Since my marriage?

HEDDA: Yes.

MRS. ELVSTED: Five years.

HEDDA: That's right. It must be.

MRS. ELVSTED: Oh, those five years. Or at least the past two or three. If you only knew, Mrs. Tesman.

HEDDA: *(taps her hand slightly)* Mrs. Tesman? Hedda! Hedda!

MRS. ELVSTED: Yes, all right, I'm sorry. I'll try.... If only you knew, Hedda, if only you could just understand....

HEDDA: *(casually)* Eilert Løvborg lived up there near you too, didn't he? During the past two or three years.

MRS. ELVSTED: Eilert Løvborg? *(looks at her uncertainly)* Yes. Yes, he did.

HEDDA: Did you know him before—when he lived in town?

MRS. ELVSTED: Oh, not really. Hardly at all. I mean, I knew his name, of course.

HEDDA: But up there—you must have seen him quite often...?

MRS. ELVSTED: Yes. He came to the house every day. He was tutoring the children, you know. Because, well, what with everything else—I couldn't do it myself.

HEDDA: Of course not. And your husband? He must have to be away from home quite often?

MRS. ELVSTED: Well, yes, Mrs. Tes— Hedda, as a

34

public official he has to travel all over the district.

HEDDA: Thea—my poor, sweet Thea—now you must tell me everything—just as it is.

MRS. ELVSTED: I—no—you had better ask the questions.

HEDDA: Well, what sort of man is your husband? I mean—to be with, live with.... What's he like? Is he good to you?

MRS. ELVSTED: *(evasively)* I'm sure he thinks he does everything for the best.

HEDDA: But he's rather too old for you, isn't he? At least twenty years older than you, I believe.

MRS. ELVSTED: *(irritated)* That's true. Along with everything else. If the truth be told, I ... I—he disgusts me. We have not a thing in common. Not a single thing.

HEDDA: But he must be fond of you. I mean, in his own way.

MRS. ELVSTED: I don't know. I think he thinks of me as ... useful to him. I don't spend much money. I'm ... inexpensive.

HEDDA: More fool you.

MRS. ELVSTED: *(shaking her head)* There's no option. Not with him. He thinks only of himself—and perhaps the children. A little.

HEDDA: And Eilert Løvborg, Thea?

MRS. ELVSTED: Eilert Løvborg? What makes you say that?

HEDDA: Well, when he sends you all the way to town to look after him ... it seems to me....

35

(smiles, almost imperceptibly) Besides, that's what you told my husband. . . .

MRS. ELVSTED: Did I? *(nervous gesture)* Yes, I suppose I did. *(quiet outburst)* No—I might as well tell you here and now. . . . It's bound to come out anyway sooner or later.

HEDDA: But my dear Thea. . . ?

MRS. ELVSTED: All right. My husband doesn't know that I'm here.

HEDDA: What? He doesn't know?!

MRS. ELVSTED: No. He wasn't home. He's gone away again—oh, I couldn't stand it any longer, Hedda. It . . . it's become impossible. I'm all alone up there. I packed a few of my things—just those that I needed—I said nothing to anyone. And I left.

HEDDA: Just like that.

MRS. ELVSTED: Yes. And I took the first train to town.

HEDDA: But my dear Thea . . . how could you bring yourself to do a thing like that?

MRS. ELVSTED: *(rises, pauses)* What else could I do?

HEDDA: But what will he say. . . ? When you go back home.

MRS. ELVSTED: *(by table, looks at her)* Go back? To him?

HEDDA: Yes.

MRS. ELVSTED: I'll never go back.

HEDDA: *(rises, approaches slowly)* So you've left him. For good.

MRS. ELVSTED: Yes. There was nothing else to do.

HEDDA: But...to go away, so—so openly.

MRS. ELVSTED: You can't keep a thing like that secret.

HEDDA: But what do you think people will say, Thea?

MRS. ELVSTED: God knows, they can say what they like. *(Sitting on sofa. Sad. Tired.)* I only did what I had to do.

HEDDA: *(brief silence)* What do you intend to do now? Will you find work?

MRS. ELVSTED: I don't know yet. All I know is, I have to live here, near Eilert Løvborg, if I am to live at all.

HEDDA: *(moves chair from table, sits beside her, strokes her hands)* Thea—tell me—how did this—this friendship between you and Eilert Løvborg—how did it begin?

MRS. ELVSTED: It just happened. Little by little. I had some sort of power over him, I suppose.

HEDDA: Oh?

MRS. ELVSTED: He gave up his old habits. Not because I asked him to. I couldn't do that. But he knew that they upset me. So he just stopped.

HEDDA: *(quickly hiding a scornful smile)* So you have—rehabilitated him, as they say. My dear Thea!

MRS. ELVSTED: That's what he says. And he has done something for me. He's made me feel like a human being again. Taught me to think—to understand things that before...so many things...

HEDDA: A tutor to you as well as to the children?

MRS. ELVSTED: No, not exactly. But he'd talk to me—for hours. About so many things. And then it became truly beautiful. I was so happy— he let me share in his work. He let me help him.

HEDDA: He did?

MRS. ELVSTED: Yes. When he was writing the book— we—we would work on it together.

HEDDA: Like the best of friends!

MRS. ELVSTED: Yes. Oh, yes. That's how he felt, too. Oh, Hedda, just think—I ought to be so happy. But I'm not. I'm so afraid it won't last.

HEDDA: You don't trust him any more than that?

MRS. ELVSTED: There's always been the shadow of another woman. She stands between Eilert Løvborg and me.

HEDDA: *(very intent)* Who?

MRS. ELVSTED: I don't know. A shadow from his past. Someone he can't forget.

HEDDA: What has he told you—about this?

MRS. ELVSTED: He brought it up only once—in passing. That's all.

HEDDA: And what did he say?

MRS. ELVSTED: He said that when they broke up she threatened to kill him. With a gun.

HEDDA: *(cold, restrained)* Nonsense. Not here! People just don't do that sort of thing.

MRS. ELVSTED: No. That's true. That's why I thought it might just have been that singer he used to—the one with the red hair—?

HEDDA: That's possible.

MRS. ELVSTED: People said she carried a gun.

HEDDA: It was probably her. It must have been.

MRS. ELVSTED: *(wringing her hands)* She's come back—oh, Hedda—that's what I've heard. She's come back. I'm in despair, Hedda!

HEDDA: Shhh! *(glances at inner room)* Here's Tesman— *(gets up and whispers)* Not a word! To anybody.

MRS. ELVSTED: *(jumps up)* No! No, of course!

(Tesman enters, letter in hand, from right)

TESMAN: There we are—all finished.

HEDDA: Good. Mrs. Elvsted was just leaving. If you wait a moment I'll walk you to the gate.

TESMAN: Hedda, dear—do you think Berte could take care of this?

HEDDA: *(takes letter)* I'll see to it.

(Berte enters from hall)

BERTE: Judge Brack is here. He wonders if he might see you both, ma'am?

HEDDA: Yes. Ask the Judge to come in. And—here—put this in the mailbox, would you?

BERTE: *(takes letter)* Yes, ma'am.

(Opens door for Judge Brack. Exits. Judge Brack is forty-five. Thickset. Well built. Brisk. Graceful. Round face. Distinguished profile. Short hair, mostly black. Well groomed. Eyes bright, sparkling. Thick eyebrows and moustache. Well-tailored walking suit. Pince-nez on string, which he lets fall on occasion.)

JUDGE BRACK: *(hat in hand, bowing)* May one pay one's respects so early in the morning?

HEDDA: One certainly may.

TESMAN: *(shakes hand)* You're always welcome here. *(introducing him)* Judge Brack—Mrs. Rysing.

HEDDA: *(quiet groan)* Ahh....

BRACK: *(bows)* Delighted!

HEDDA: *(looks at him and laughs)* It's a pleasure to see you in daylight, Judge Brack.

BRACK: Have I changed?

HEDDA: A bit younger, I think.

BRACK: Thank you.

TESMAN: But look at my Hedda, hmm? Doesn't she have a kind of glow to her, hmm? She's positively...

HEDDA: Stop it. Please don't talk about me that way. You might thank the Judge for all the trouble he's gone to.

BRACK: Nonsense. It was a pleasure.

HEDDA: Thank you. You are a true friend. But I'm sorry, Thea, I know you have to leave. Excuse me; I'll be right back.

(Mutual goodbyes. Mrs. Elvsted and Hedda exit right.)

BRACK: Well, your wife is reasonably satisfied, I take it.

TESMAN: Oh, yes. We can't thank you enough. Of course, I understand that there are still some minor adjustments to be made. And we still need one or two things for the house. A few small purchases. Here and there.

BRACK: Oh? Really?

TESMAN: But we don't want to bother you with such things. Hedda said she'd take care of them. But...do sit down, hmm?

BRACK: Thank you. Just for a moment. *(sits by table)* There *is* something I need to talk to you about, Tesman.

TESMAN: Hmm? Oh, yes, I see. *(sits)* The time for serious financial advice. Ready for the lecture.

BRACK: Oh, no—the financial arrangements are, um...there's no great rush as far as the money's concerned.... Although I wish we could have been a little more economical.

TESMAN: That, my dear Judge, was not possible. It's all in Hedda's hands and, well, you know how she is. I couldn't let her live like a grocer's wife, now, could I?

BRACK: No. No. I understand. That *is* the problem, I suppose.

TESMAN: Besides—fortunately, it can't be long before I get my appointment.

BRACK: Well, you know, these things can take time.

TESMAN: Have you heard something? Is there any news, hmm?

BRACK: No, I've heard nothing. But—by the way—I do have something to tell you.

TESMAN: Oh?

BRACK: Your old friend Eilert Løvborg is back in town.

TESMAN: I know.

41

BRACK: Oh? Who told you?

TESMAN: The lady who was just here.

BRACK: Oh, I see. What was her name again? I didn't quite catch...

TESMAN: Mrs. Elvsted.

BRACK: Ah, yes, the sheriff's wife. Yes, he was living near them for a while.

TESMAN: And, um—so I gather—he's reformed, completely changed his ways.

BRACK: Yes, that's what they're saying.

TESMAN: And he's published a new book, hmm?

BRACK: Yes.

TESMAN: And it's caused quite a sensation.

BRACK: An extraordinary sensation.

TESMAN: Who'd have thought? Well, that's just marvelous. Isn't it? He was so very talented. I was afraid that he was done for. Finished.

BRACK: Yes. That's what everybody thought.

TESMAN: But what will he do now? Hmm? How can he possibly make a living?

(Hedda enters during Tesman's last words)

HEDDA: *(to Brack, laughing, touch of sarcasm)* Tesman is always worrying about how people are going to make a living.

TESMAN: Yes, well, my dear, we are talking about poor Eilert Løvborg.

HEDDA: *(quick glance)* Oh, really? *(sits in easy chair at stove)* What's the matter with him?

TESMAN: Well, I'm sure he's spent his inheritance—run through it long ago. And he can't write a new book every year, can he now? So I was asking how he could possibly survive.

BRACK: Perhaps I can shed a little light on that.

TESMAN: Oh?

BRACK: First, he has relatives of some considerable influence.

TESMAN: Yes, but they washed their hands of him a long time ago.

BRACK: All the same, they used to think of him as the great hope of that family.

TESMAN: Used to, but he put an end to that himself.

HEDDA: Who can say? *(smiles)* I hear that the Elvsteds have—rehabilitated him.

BRACK: Second, there's his book—

TESMAN: Well, I hope they can help him find *something* to do. I just wrote him a letter. Hedda, I asked him to come by this evening.

BRACK: Oh. That's a pity. You're supposed to join me for dinner at the club, Tesman. You'd forgotten. We talked about it last night on the pier.

HEDDA: Had you forgotten, Tesman?

TESMAN: Yes. I'm sorry. It slipped my mind.

BRACK: Well, I'm sure he won't come. So that's that!

TESMAN: Why? What makes you say that?

BRACK: *(gets up, hesitates, hands on back of chair)* My dear Tesman—and, indeed, you too, Mrs. Tesman—I cannot, in good conscience, allow us to go any further without telling you—the fact is... the fact...

HEDDA: It's Eilert Løvborg, isn't it?

TESMAN: The fact is—? Judge, please continue.

BRACK: You must face the fact that—that your appointment may not come through as quickly as you'd hoped. Or expected.

TESMAN: *(getting up quickly)* Why? Why? Has something gone wrong?

BRACK: There is a strong possibility that the appointment will be made only after a competition is held.

TESMAN: A competition? Hedda! Just think of that.

HEDDA: *(leaning back in her chair)* Yes. Yes, I see.

TESMAN: But with whom? Not with—

BRACK: Yes. With Eilert Løvborg.

TESMAN: *(striking his hands together)* No. That is out of the question. Quite impossible.

BRACK: All the same—it may well happen.

TESMAN: Yes, but, Judge, that would be unbelievably unfair. *(gesturing with his arms)* Cruel, even! After all, I'm a married man! We got married because the position was virtually promised. We went into debt. Borrowed money from Aunt Julie. The position was—was, well, virtually promised to me.

BRACK: Well, I'm sure that you'll get it in the end. But there will be a competition.

HEDDA: *(motionless in the armchair)* Just think, Tesman—a duel to the death.

44

TESMAN: How can you sit there—as if you didn't care...?

HEDDA: Oh, I care. I care deeply. I can't wait to see how it turns out.

BRACK: In any case, Mrs. Tesman, now you know how things stand. That's a minor relief to me. *(smiles)* What I mean is—those "few things" you were going to buy? That little threat is out of the question, hmm?

HEDDA: This changes nothing.

BRACK: I see. Well, that's something else again.... Goodbye. *(to Tesman)* When I take my afternoon walk, I'll call for you.

TESMAN: What? Oh, yes, please do. Yes—I'm sorry, I'm afraid I'm a little bit lost at the moment.

HEDDA: *(remains seated, gives her hand)* Goodbye, Judge. Come back soon, won't you?

BRACK: I will. Thank you. Goodbye. Goodbye.

TESMAN: *(accompanying him only to door)* Goodbye, my dear Judge. You must excuse me....

(Brack exits)

TESMAN: Oh, Hedda, Hedda. One should never live in a dream world.

HEDDA: Do *you* do that?

TESMAN: Well, yes—of course. I can't deny it. To get married—to set up a home—on the strength of a mere promise.

HEDDA: Perhaps you're right.

TESMAN: Well, at least we *have* a home—a nice, comfortable home. The home that we *both* dreamed of, Hedda. That we set our hearts on.

45

HEDDA: *(rises slowly, wearily)* Yes, that was part of our agreement—that we'd maintain a life of elegant respectability—live here—

TESMAN: I know, I know. Dearest Hedda—I have longed to see you, as the lady of this house, entertaining a select circle of our friends. Yes, well—for a while we'll just have to be by ourselves. Perhaps we'll see Aunt Julie once in a while. That's all. But I wanted it to be so different—for you, so very different.

HEDDA: I suppose a butler is now out of the question.

TESMAN: I'm afraid so. No, there's not a chance of that, under the circumstances.

HEDDA: And my horse, my own riding horse...

TESMAN: *(aghast)* The horse!

HEDDA: I suppose that is out of the question.

TESMAN: Good Lord—no—that goes without saying.

HEDDA: *(crossing room)* Well, at least I have one thing left to keep me amused.

TESMAN: *(smiling)* Well, thank heaven for that. What is it, my love, hmm?

HEDDA: *(in the doorway, with veiled scorn)* My pistols, Jørgen.

TESMAN: *(afraid)* Your pistols.

HEDDA: *(cold stare)* General Gabler's pistols. *(she exits through inner door)*

TESMAN: *(to doorway, calling after her)* No, Hedda! For heaven's sake.... Please! Don't touch them! Leave them alone. For my sake, Hedda. Please.

ACT 2

The same room, but the piano has been removed. In its place is an elegant little writing table. A small table, new sofa. Most of the flowers have been removed. Mrs. Elv sted's bouquet is on the center table. It is afternoon. Hedda is dressed to receive callers. She stands alone near the open French windows, loading a revolver. The other is lying in an open case on the desk.

HEDDA: *(looking into garden, calls out)* Good afternoon, Judge! Welcome back!

BRACK: *(from garden)* Thank you, Mrs. Tesman.

HEDDA: *(raises pistol)* Judge Brack, your time has come!

BRACK: *(still in garden)* No! No! No! Don't point it at me.

HEDDA: That's what you get for sneaking in round the back. *(fires)*

BRACK: *(nearer)* Are you out of your mind?

HEDDA: Oh, dear—I didn't hit you, did I?

BRACK: *(still outside)* Stop it. Stop this nonsense.

HEDDA: All right. Do come in.

BRACK: *(Dressed for dinner. Enters, carrying a light overcoat.)* Good God, woman! Are you still playing your ridiculous games? What are you shooting at?

HEDDA: Oh, I was just firing into the blue of the sky.

BRACK: *(gently taking the gun)* If you'll permit me, Mrs. Tesman. *(looks at it)* Ah, yes, I remember this very well. *(looks around)* Where is the case? Ah, here we are. *(puts gun in case, closes it)* We'll have no more of that nonsense this afternoon.

HEDDA: Well, what in God's name am I supposed to do with myself?

BRACK: No visitors?

HEDDA: *(closing glass door)* No. Not one. I suppose all our friends are still out of town.

BRACK: And Tesman? Not at home?

HEDDA: *(at writing table, puts pistol case in drawer)* No. After lunch he went off to see his aunts. He didn't expect you back so soon.

BRACK: I should have thought of that. That was stupid of me.

HEDDA: *(turning to him)* Stupid? Why?

BRACK: If I'd known, I'd have come by even earlier.

HEDDA: *(crossing room)* If you had, you wouldn't have found anyone at home. I was in my room, getting dressed.

BRACK: Ah! And there isn't a small crack in the door for us to—to converse through?

HEDDA: You forgot to see to that.

BRACK: Also stupid of me.

HEDDA: So we'll have to stay right here. And wait. ... I don't think Tesman will be back for a while.

BRACK: I can be very patient.

(Hedda sits on sofa. Brack puts overcoat on nearby chair—sits. Keeps his hat. Brief pause. They look at one another.)

HEDDA: Well?

BRACK: *(imitates her tone)* Well?

HEDDA: I said it first.

BRACK: All right. *(leans forward)* Let's have a nice, quiet chat, Mrs.— Hedda Gabler. *(leans back)*

HEDDA: It seems like a lifetime since we last talked together. Doesn't it? I don't mean last night or this morning. That meant nothing.

BRACK: You mean—just the two of us. Alone.

HEDDA: Something like that.

BRACK: I missed you. Every day you were gone.

HEDDA: I felt the same way.

BRACK: Did you? Honestly? I thought you were having a marvelous time.

HEDDA: Marvelous.

BRACK: That's what Tesman said in his letters.

HEDDA: Oh, yes. It was marvelous for him. He loved poking around in collections of old books. Copying his—his parchments, or whatever you call them.

BRACK: *(with a smile)* But that's what he does. Isn't it? Partly, anyway.

HEDDA: Yes. That's what he does. And there's nothing wrong with it—but what about *me*? Oh, Judge—you just don't know. I'm so terribly bored.

BRACK: *(sympathetically)* Are you? In all seriousness?

HEDDA: You must understand—to go away for months on end. No one to talk to. No one who knew our circle of friends, or who was interested in my kind of life.

BRACK: Yes, I believe I would have been bored, too.

HEDDA: And the most unbearable thing of all—

BRACK: What?

HEDDA: To be with the same person...all the... everlastingly.

BRACK: Morning, noon, and night. Yes—I do understand. At every conceivable hour.

HEDDA: I said everlastingly.

BRACK: I understand. Still, Tesman is such a good man—I should have thought.

HEDDA: My dear Judge—Tesman is an academic.

BRACK: True.

HEDDA: And academics are not the most entertaining traveling companions. Not in the long run, anyway.

BRACK: Not even the academic one loves?

HEDDA: Don't use that nauseating word.

BRACK: *(puzzled)* I don't understand, Mrs. Tesman.

HEDDA: *(half laughing, half annoyed)* You should try it sometime. Listening to the cultural history of civilization. Morning, noon, and night.

BRACK: Everlastingly.

HEDDA: Yes. Yes! And the Middle Ages, and the cottage industries of the Brabant—Oh, God!

BRACK: *(looks at her closely)* Then how...how did you...I mean...

HEDDA: Why did I choose Jørgen Tesman?

BRACK: If you want to put it that way, yes.

HEDDA: Oh, come now. Do you really find that so strange?

BRACK: Well, yes—and in some ways, no.

HEDDA: I was tired of the dance. Tired. My time was over. *(with a shudder)* No, I don't want to say that. I don't want to think it.

BRACK: No. There's no reason to. None at all.

HEDDA: Oh, reasons—reasons. *(watching him)* And, anyway, Jørgen Tesman is a perfectly respectable young man.

BRACK: Perfectly. And absolutely dependable.

HEDDA: And there's nothing about him that one could call slightly—ridiculous?

BRACK: Ridiculous....No. I wouldn't say that.

HEDDA: And what's more—he works unbelievably hard on his research. There's no doubt about that. In time he may go very far.

BRACK: I assumed that you, like everyone else, believed in him, believed indeed that he would become an eminent scholar.

HEDDA: *(tired)* Yes, I did. And then when he insisted that he wanted to take care of me—provide for me. What could I do but accept?

BRACK: No, of course—if you look at it that way....

HEDDA: That was more than my other admirers were willing to do for me.

51

BRACK: *(laughs)* Well, I can't speak for all of them. ...But as far as I am concerned—I've always had a great deal of respect for the institution of marriage. Always—in general, that is, Mrs. Tesman.

HEDDA: *(teasing)* Well, I never really had any high hopes for you.

BRACK: All I want is a close circle of intimate friends—I want to be of use—I want to help—to come and go simply as a friend—a trusted friend.

HEDDA: You mean, of the master of the house.

BRACK: *(bowing slightly)* To be perfectly honest—I meant the lady. But the master, too, of course. That kind of triangle of friends—*à trois,* shall we say—can be wonderfully satisfying for all concerned.

HEDDA: Yes, there were many times that I wanted someone else with us. Oh, those endless conversations in the railway carriages. Just the two of us.

BRACK: Fortunately, the wedding trip is over.

HEDDA: *(shaking her head)* No, there's a long way to go. I've just come to the first stop on the line.

BRACK: Well, at the station you get out, move around, and...

HEDDA: I'll never get out.

BRACK: Never?

HEDDA: No. There's always someone who...

BRACK: *(laughs)* Looks at one's legs, is that it?

HEDDA: Yes. Exactly.

BRACK: But, after all, what's the...

HEDDA: *(cutting him off)* Never. That's not for me. I shall keep my seat. I will not move. Just the two of us.

BRACK: But what if a third party were to come in and join you?

HEDDA: Ah! That would be quite different.

BRACK: A friend. A trusted friend.

HEDDA: An entertaining friend. Full of life.

BRACK: And not an academic.

HEDDA: *(with a sigh)* Yes. Oh, yes, that would be a relief.

BRACK: *(hearing door open)* We are now *à trois*.

HEDDA: *(quietly)* And the train goes on.

(Tesman enters. Grey walking suit. Felt hat. Pile of books in hands. Others in his pockets.)

TESMAN: *(to table, breathing with the weight)* Oh, this is quite a load to carry.... And it's so hot out. *(puts books down)* I'm sweating—oh, Judge! I'm sorry. I didn't know you were here. Berte didn't tell me.

BRACK: *(rises)* I came in through the garden.

HEDDA: What are all those books?

TESMAN: *(stands leafing through some of them)* New publications—in my special field.

HEDDA: Special field.

BRACK: Yes, Mrs. Tesman—special field.

(they smile)

53

HEDDA: What do you need them for?

TESMAN: My dear Hedda, as a specialist I need every book, every article that's published in my field. I have to keep up with all the current literature.

HEDDA: I'm sure you're right.

TESMAN: *(searching through)* Look. Here's Løvborg's new book. Did you want to see it, Hedda? *(offers it)*

HEDDA: No—thank you. Perhaps later.

TESMAN: I took a quick look at it on the way home.

BRACK: And what do you—as a specialist—what do you think of it?

TESMAN: It's actually quite remarkable. Serious, thoughtful, precise. He's never written like this before. *(gathers books)* But—if you'll excuse me— I'll take these into the study. I can't wait to cut the pages. And then I'll change for dinner. We're not late, are we?

BRACK: No. Not at all. There's plenty of time.

TESMAN: Well, in that case, I won't rush. *(starts out, stops in doorway)* Oh, by the way, Hedda—Aunt Julie won't be coming over this evening.

HEDDA: Oh, really? Is she still upset about the hat?

TESMAN: Oh, no! Aunt Julie's not like that. Really, Hedda! No. It's Aunt Rina—she's very ill.

HEDDA: Isn't she always?

TESMAN: Yes, but today she really took a turn for the worse.

HEDDA: Then she's right to stay with her. I'll just have to put up with it. That's all.

TESMAN: Aunt Julie was, in fact, delighted with her visit this morning. She thought you looked the picture of health.

HEDDA: *(under her breath, rising)* Oh, these infernal aunts.

TESMAN: Hmm?

HEDDA: *(to French doors)* Nothing.

TESMAN: Oh, well, all right. Excuse me— *(exits right)*

BRACK: What happened with the hat?

HEDDA: Oh, nothing—it was—Miss Tesman—this morning. She'd put her hat down on that chair. *(she smiles)* And I pretended to think it was the maid's.

BRACK: *(shaking his head)* My dear Hedda—how could you do that? She's such a sweet lady.

HEDDA: *(nervous—pacing)* Sometimes I can't help myself. I just do things...all of a sudden...on a whim. *(sits in armchair by stove)* Oh, I can't explain it.

BRACK: You're not really happy....*(behind his chair)* That's the truth, isn't it?

HEDDA: *(staring straight ahead)* I know of no reason why I should be happy—do you?

BRACK: Well, yes—among other things—you have the home that you always wanted.

HEDDA: Ah, you too! You too believe this house was my one great passion. *(looks at him, laughs)*

BRACK: You mean, it wasn't true?

HEDDA: Perhaps there was some truth in it.

BRACK: And?

HEDDA: Tesman used to escort me home last summer—after our dinner parties—

BRACK: Unfortunately, I had to take a different path.

HEDDA: Yes, you took quite a different path last summer.

BRACK: *(laughs)* Mrs. Tesman! Shame on you.... Anyway, go on about Tesman.

HEDDA: We passed by here one evening and—Tesman was a nervous wreck as usual, trying to think of something to talk about—and I felt sorry for him—for this intellectual....

BRACK: Honestly? *(doubting smile)* Did you?

HEDDA: I really did. So, there was this awkward silence—and again, just on a whim—I broke it by saying that I'd like to live in this house.

BRACK: Just like that?

HEDDA: Just like that.

BRACK: And then?

HEDDA: And then, my whimsicality had its consequences.

BRACK: As it often does, Mrs. Tesman. For all of us.

HEDDA: Thank you. So you see, Tesman and I found each other in our common passion for the house of Senator Falk. Then there was the engagement and the wedding and the honeymoon and—all the rest of it.... I was going to say I've made my bed—now I must lie in it....

BRACK: Priceless, Hedda. Priceless. *(pause)* But then, this house means virtually nothing to you?

HEDDA: Oh, God, no.

BRACK: Not even now? After all, we've done what you asked for—it's elegant, comfortable.

HEDDA: *(expression of disgust)* All the rooms reek of lavender and rose petals. Perhaps that's Aunt Julie's fault. She brought it with her.

BRACK: *(laughing)* No, I think that's a bouquet from the late Mrs. Falk.

HEDDA: Yes, there is a smell of mortality about it. Like a corsage the morning after. *(hands behind her neck, leaning back, looks at him)* Oh, Judge—you cannot conceive how unutterably bored I shall be out here.

BRACK: There must be something you can do to make life more interesting—Let us call it a . . . distraction.

HEDDA: Something . . . to bring me pleasure.

BRACK: Precisely.

HEDDA: I can't imagine what that could be. However, I often wonder whether— *(interrupting herself)* But it won't come to anything either.

BRACK: Who can say? Tell me what it is.

HEDDA: I wonder whether I couldn't get Tesman interested in a political career.

BRACK: *(laughs)* Tesman! No, my dear, a political life is not for him. He's entirely unsuited.

HEDDA: I'm sure you're right. But all the same, couldn't I ease him in that direction? Make him take it up?

BRACK: No doubt. But what would be your satisfaction if he were to fail? Why would you have him do that?

HEDDA: Because I'm bored.... I've told you. *(after a pause)* Do you think it absolutely impossible for Tesman to become, say, a cabinet minister?

BRACK: Hmm. You see, my dear Hedda, for him to acquire such a position he would have to be a comparatively wealthy man.

HEDDA: *(rising impatiently)* Yes. That's it exactly. This...this poverty that I've come into. *(crosses room)* That's what makes my life so miserable. So totally...absurd. Yes. For that's what it is.

BRACK: I disagree. I don't think it's that at all.

HEDDA: What then?

BRACK: I don't think you've ever lived through anything that...that has challenged you.

HEDDA: Anything truly serious, you mean?

BRACK: You could put it that way. But it may be about to happen.

HEDDA: If you mean this wretched business about the professorship—that's Tesman's problem, not mine. I shan't give it a second thought.

BRACK: No, it's not that. Suppose—to put it as delicately as possible, you were to find yourself carrying a greater responsibility? Some new claim upon our little Mrs. Tesman?

HEDDA: *(angry)* Be quiet! You will never see anything like that happen. Never.

BRACK: *(cautiously)* We'll talk about that in a year's time...hmm? At the most.

HEDDA: *(curtly)* I have no plans of that kind, Judge Brack. Nothing that will lay claim to me.

BRACK: Ah. But shouldn't you? After all, most women have the need, the desire...

HEDDA: I told you to be quiet. *(by the door)* I have often thought that I have only one need, one desire.

BRACK: *(approaching her)* And what is that—if I may be so bold?

HEDDA: To bore myself to death. There. Now you know. *(turns, looks back at room, and laughs)* You see! Here's the proof. Our professor!

BRACK: *(softly, in a warning voice)* Now, now, Hedda!

(Tesman, in evening dress with hat and gloves, enters from inner room)

TESMAN: Hedda? Any word from Eilert Løvborg? Hmm?

HEDDA: No. Nothing yet.

TESMAN: Well, I expect he'll be here soon.

HEDDA: Do you really think he'll come?

TESMAN: Certain of it. *(to Brack)* I feel sure that what you told us this morning... was just gossip—rumor.

BRACK: You think so?

TESMAN: That's what Aunt Julie thinks, at any rate. She's absolutely certain that he won't stand in my way. Think of that.

BRACK: Ah, well. That's good to hear.

TESMAN: *(Puts hat and gloves on chair, right. To Brack.)*

59

But, if you don't mind, I'd like to wait for him as long as possible.

BRACK: There's plenty of time. There'll be no one there until seven or seven-thirty.

TESMAN: So, in the meantime, we can keep Hedda company, hmm? While we wait.

HEDDA: *(takes Brack's hat and coat to sofa)* If worst comes to worst, Mr. Løvborg can stay and talk to me.

BRACK: *(trying to take his hat and coat)* Allow me, Mrs. Tesman. What do you mean—if worst comes to worst?

HEDDA: If he doesn't want to go with you and Tesman.

TESMAN: *(looking at her, dubious)* Now, Hedda, dear—I don't think that would be, um, proper, do you? After all, Aunt Julie isn't going to be coming.

HEDDA: No, but Mrs. Elvsted will be here. The three of us will have tea together.

TESMAN: Yes, well, I'm sure that will be all right.

BRACK: *(smiling)* It's probably the safest thing to do, anyway.

HEDDA: What do you mean?

BRACK: Well, if you remember, Mrs. Tesman, you always used to... show a certain disdain for my parties. You said they were only fit for gentle-men—gentlemen of the highest principles.

HEDDA: No doubt Mr. Løvborg's principles are high enough now. The reformed sinner...

(Berte appears at hall door)

BERTE: There's a gentleman at the door, ma'am. He's asking if you're at home.

HEDDA: Show him in.

TESMAN: *(quietly)* I'm sure that's him. Think of that!

(Eilert Løvborg enters from the hall. He is slim, wiry. Same age as Tesman but looks older, haggard. Tired. His hair and beard are dark brown. Face long, pale, patches of color on the cheekbones. Dressed in new black visiting suit. Dark gloves, silk hat. Stops at door, makes a quick bow. Seems embarrassed.)

TESMAN: *(shaking him by the hand, warmly)* Well, well, my dear Eilert—it's been such a long time.

LØVBORG: *(subdued voice)* Thank you for your letter, Tesman. *(going to her)* And may I shake your hand, too, Mrs. Tesman?

HEDDA: *(taking his hand)* I am pleased to see you, Mr. Løvborg. *(motioning an introduction)* I don't know whether you two gentlemen...

LØVBORG: *(slight bow)* Judge Brack, I believe.

BRACK: *(slight bow)* Yes—it's been quite some time.

TESMAN: *(placing his hands on Løvborg's shoulders)* Now then, I want you to feel right at home here. He must—mustn't he, Hedda? Especially since I hear you're coming back to live in town, hmm?

LØVBORG: Yes. Yes, I am.

TESMAN: Well, that makes sense, hmm, Hedda? Listen, I've just got a copy of your new book— haven't had time to read it yet.

LØVBORG: Save yourself the trouble.

TESMAN: Why? What do you mean?

61

LØVBORG: There's nothing much to it, really.

TESMAN: Good heavens, man—how can you say that?

BRACK: But it's been received very well, I gather. Much praised.

LØVBORG: Well, that's all I really wanted. So I put nothing into the book that was even remotely controversial.

BRACK: Very clever.

TESMAN: Well, but, my dear Eilert...

LØVBORG: No. You see, I intend to get this new appointment—make a fresh start.

TESMAN: *(slightly embarrassed)* Yes. Yes. I see. There is that to consider.

LØVBORG: *(smiling, lays down hat, and takes a packet wrapped in paper from his coat pocket)* Now, when this is published, Tesman, you will have to read it. This is the real book. I have put myself—all of myself—into these pages.

TESMAN: Indeed? And what is it?

LØVBORG: The sequel.

TESMAN: To what?

LØVBORG: The book.

TESMAN: Your new one?

LØVBORG: Of course.

TESMAN: Yes, but I thought that you had already— in your analysis—covered contemporary history.

LØVBORG: I have. This one deals with the future of civilization.

TESMAN: Yes, but we can know nothing about the future.

LØVBORG: No, but there are one or two things that one can say about it, nonetheless. *(opens packet)* Take a look—

TESMAN: That's not your handwriting, is it?

LØVBORG: I dictated it. *(flipping through pages)* It's in two parts. The first is an analysis of potential civilizing forces. And the second *(running through the end pages)* is a projection of the probable lines of development.

TESMAN: That's so very strange. I would never have thought of writing anything like that.

HEDDA: *(at glass door, drumming on window pane)* Probably not.

LØVBORG: *(replacing manuscript in package and laying it on table)* I had hoped that I might read you some of it this evening.

TESMAN: That was very good of you, Løvborg. But this evening...*(looks at Brack)* I don't see how we can....

LØVBORG: Well then, some other time. It can wait.

BRACK: You see, I'm giving a small dinner party this evening—mainly in Tesman's honor.

LØVBORG: *(looking for hat)* Then I won't detain you.

BRACK: No, no. It would be delightful if you'd join us.

LØVBORG: *(curtly)* No, that's not possible. But thank you.

BRACK: Oh, come along. It's a small intimate gath-

ering. We shall have a "gay old time" as Hed—
Mrs. Tesman would say.

LØVBORG: I'm sure you will. However, it's not...

BRACK: And you could bring the manuscript with
you and read it to Tesman later—at my house. I
could give you a room to yourselves.

TESMAN: That's very kind of you. What do you
think, Eilert? Why don't you, hmm?

HEDDA: I think it's clear, Tesman, that Mr. Løvborg
would prefer not to go. I'm sure he is more
inclined to stay here and have supper with me.

LØVBORG: With you, Mrs. Tesman? *(looking at her)*

HEDDA: And Mrs. Elvsted.

LØVBORG: Ah—*(passing it off lightly)* Yes, I happened
to see her for a moment this morning.

HEDDA: Did you? Well, she is coming this evening. So, you see, you must stay, Mr. Løvborg.
Otherwise, she will have no one to see her
home.

LØVBORG: I suppose that's true. Thank you, Mrs.
Tesman—in that case, I shall stay.

HEDDA: Then will you please excuse me for a
moment—I have to speak to the maid. *(Goes to
hall door. Rings bell. Enter Berte. Hedda whispers to
her, points to inner room. Berte nods and leaves.)*

TESMAN: *(during this exchange)* Tell me, Eilert—this
new field of yours—this analysis of the future—
is that what you are going to lecture about?

LØVBORG: Yes.

TESMAN: When I was at the bookstore, they told

me you are going to give a series of lectures in the autumn.

LØVBORG: That is my intention, yes. I hope, Tesman, that will not upset you in any way.

TESMAN: No. No. Not in the least. But, um...

LØVBORG: I quite understand that it can bring you no pleasure.

TESMAN: *(uncomfortable)* Well, I could hardly expect you—out of consideration for me—to, um...

LØVBORG: I shall wait, however, until you have received your appointment.

TESMAN: You'll wait? Yes, but...but aren't you going to comp— aren't you going to apply for the position?

LØVBORG: No. It's only the moral victory that I care for.

TESMAN: Good Lord.... Aunt Julie was right after all. I knew it—Hedda! Just think. Eilert has no intention of standing in our way.

HEDDA: Our way? *(coldly)* Please leave me out of this. *(She goes to door of inner room. Berte is placing a tray with decanter and glasses on the table. Hedda nods approval and comes back again. Berte leaves.)*

TESMAN: *(during the above)* And you, Judge Brack, hmm? What do you have to say about this?

BRACK: Well, a moral victory...yes...a moral victory has its virtues, but all the same...

TESMAN: Yes, of course—but all the same...

HEDDA: *(looking at Tesman with a cold smile)* You look as though you've been struck by lightning.

65

TESMAN: Yes, well, so I have, I almost think.

BRACK: Don't you see, Mrs. Tesman? A thunderstorm has just passed over us.

HEDDA: *(indicating inner room)* Will you take a glass of cold punch, gentlemen?

BRACK: A glass of punch? *(looking at his watch)* Yes. Thank you. That would be a pleasure.

TESMAN: Excellent idea, Hedda! Just the thing! Now that the weight has been taken off my mind. . . .

HEDDA: Won't you join them, Mr. Løvborg?

LØVBORG: *(gesture of refusal)* No. No, thank you. Nothing for me.

BRACK: Good heavens, man—cold punch! It's not poison.

LØVBORG: No—not for others.

HEDDA: I will keep Mr. Løvborg company while you take your drink.

TESMAN: Yes. Yes, Hedda dear, do—thank you.

(He and Brack exit. They drink punch, smoke, and engage in animated conversation during the following scene. Løvborg remains standing by the stove. Hedda goes to the writing table.)

HEDDA: *(raising her voice a little)* Would you care to look at some photographs, Mr. Løvborg? Tesman and I took a trip through the Tyrol on our way home. *(Picks up album, places it on table by sofa, and sits in corner. Løvborg approaches, stops, and looks at her. Then he takes chair and seats himself to her left, with his back to the inner room.)*

66

HEDDA: *(opening album)* You see this mountain range, Mr. Løvborg? It's the Ortler group. Tesman has written the name underneath: "The Ortlers—near Meran."

LØVBORG: *(who has never taken his eyes off her—softly and slowly)* Hedda—Gabler!

HEDDA: *(glancing quickly at him)* Ah—shhh!

LØVBORG: *(again, softly)* Hedda Gabler.

HEDDA: *(looking at album)* That *was* my name—in the old days—when we two knew each other.

LØVBORG: And now I must learn never to say Hedda Gabler again—never—as long as I live.

HEDDA: Yes, you must. *(still turning the pages)* And I think you should practice it. The sooner the better.

LØVBORG: *(indignant)* Hedda Gabler—married! And married to Jørgen Tesman.

HEDDA: Yes. . . . So it goes.

LØVBORG: Oh, Hedda—Hedda—how could you throw yourself away?

HEDDA: *(looking at him sharply)* I won't allow this!

LØVBORG: What do you mean?

(Tesman enters, goes to sofa)

HEDDA: *(hears him coming and says unconcernedly)* And this is the view from the Val D'Ampezzo, Mr. Løvborg. Just look at that. *(looks affectionately up at Tesman)* What's the name of these mountains, darling?

TESMAN: Let me see. Oh. Those are the Dolomites.

HEDDA: Yes, of course. Those are the Dolomites, Mr. Løvborg.

TESMAN: Hedda, my dear, would you like a glass of punch? Just for yourself, hmm? I just came to ask.

HEDDA: Yes, I would, and perhaps some petits-fours.

TESMAN: Cigarettes?

HEDDA: No.

TESMAN: Right. *(Goes into inner room and exits right. Brack occasionally watches Hedda and Løvborg.)*

LØVBORG: *(softly, as before)* Hedda, tell me—how could you do this?

HEDDA: *(apparently absorbed in album as before)* If you persist in being so familiar with me, I shall leave.

LØVBORG: But we are alone—may I not...?

HEDDA: You may think it but not say it.

LØVBORG: I understand. I must not invade the world of Jørgen Tesman—the man you love.

HEDDA: *(smiles)* Love? *(laughs to herself)*

LØVBORG: You don't love him, then?

HEDDA: I will never be unfaithful to him. Never. Remember that.

LØVBORG: Hedda, answer me one thing—

HEDDA: Shhh!

(Tesman enters with small tray)

TESMAN: Here you are. They look tempting, don't they? *(puts tray on table)*

68

HEDDA: Why did you bring it yourself?

TESMAN: It gives me pleasure to wait on you, Hedda.

HEDDA: Why have you poured out two glasses? Mr. Løvborg said he wouldn't have any.

TESMAN: No. It was for Mrs. Elvsted. She'll be here soon, won't she?

HEDDA: Yes...Mrs. Elvsted...very soon, I expect.

TESMAN: You'd forgotten, eh?

HEDDA: We were so absorbed in the photographs. *(showing him one)* Do you remember this little village?

TESMAN: Let me see...yes. That's just below the Brenner Pass. We spent the night there.

HEDDA: And met that party of tourists.

TESMAN: That's right. That was the place. You'd have enjoyed being with us, Eilert, wouldn't he, hmm? *(returns to Brack)*

LØVBORG: Answer me this one thing, Hedda.

HEDDA: Yes.

LØVBORG: Was there no love—no flicker of love in your friendship for me?

HEDDA: I wonder if there was. I suppose I feel that we were very close—two very intimate friends. *(she smiles)* You in particular were always very—frank.

LØVBORG: You made me so.

HEDDA: When I look back on it, I think...I feel... there was something very beautiful—fascinating—even daring in that intimacy...that secret friendship of ours. No one ever knew.

LØVBORG: Yes, yes, Hedda. I feel it, too. I used to come to your father's house, in the afternoon. He'd sit by the window reading the papers, with his back to us.

HEDDA: And we sat on the sofa in the corner.

LØVBORG: With the same magazine on the table in front of us.

HEDDA: There being no photographs.

LØVBORG: No—and then, Hedda, I told you—confessed to you—things about myself...that no one else knew. At least not then. I sat there and told you openly about my—awful destructive life. About the lost days and nights. Hedda, Hedda, what power did you have over me, that you could force me to tell you those things?

HEDDA: Do you think I had power over you?

LØVBORG: What else could I think? The way you phrased your questions...so evasive...so ambiguous....

HEDDA: Which you understood so clearly.

LØVBORG: How could you sit there and question me like that? Question me quite frankly....

HEDDA: But evasively...as you pointed out.

LØVBORG: Yes, but frankly, nevertheless. Question after question—about all sorts of things.

HEDDA: And how could you answer, Mr. Løvborg?

LØVBORG: That is what I don't understand, when I look back on it. Hedda, I ask you again—was there no love, no love at all? When you made me confess to you—did you ever feel that you could absolve me of my sins? Tell me, did you?

HEDDA: No, not quite.

LØVBORG: Then why did you do it?

HEDDA: Don't you see, a young girl—given such a chance, without anyone knowing...

LØVBORG: Yes?

HEDDA: Could not resist looking in on a world which...which...

LØVBORG: Well?

HEDDA: Which is absolutely forbidden to her.

LØVBORG: So that was it?

HEDDA: Partly. Partly—at least I think so.

LØVBORG: But friendship...that is the reason for being. Why did that have to die for us?

HEDDA: The fault was yours.

LØVBORG: It was you who left me.

HEDDA: Yes, when that friendship threatened to become something more serious. *(pauses)* You had no shame. How could you think of breaking that trust—of dishonoring me?

LØVBORG: *(with clenched fists)* Then why didn't you go through with it? Why didn't you shoot me down?

HEDDA: The scandal. I was afraid of the scandal.

LØVBORG: Yes. Yes, Hedda, you were always a coward at heart.

HEDDA: A terrible coward. *(changing her tone)* Which was lucky for you. But now you have all the comfort and consolation you need. At the Elvsteds.

LØVBORG: I know that Thea has spoken to you.

HEDDA: And perhaps you have told her something about us?

LØVBORG: No. Not a word. She's too stupid to understand things like that.

HEDDA: Stupid?

LØVBORG: Yes. Stupid...about things like that.

HEDDA: And I am a coward. *(leans toward him and without looking him in the eye, says softly)* But now I shall tell you something—in confidence.

LØVBORG: *(eagerly)* Yes?

HEDDA: The fact that I did not shoot you down— that was...

LØVBORG: Yes?

HEDDA: That was not what made me a coward— that night.

LØVBORG: *(looks at her a moment, understands, and whispers passionately)* Oh, Hedda! Hedda Gabler! I begin to see now what made us such close friends. You and I—! You, too, had this passion for life—

HEDDA: *(softly, with a quick glance)* Take care! Don't think it for a moment!

(It is growing dark. Berte opens the hall door.)

HEDDA: *(snaps the album shut and calls out)* Well! At last—my dear Thea! Do come in.

(Mrs. Elvsted enters in evening dress. The door is closed behind her.)

HEDDA: *(on sofa, stretches her arms toward her)* Thea, darling, you can have no idea how I've been longing for this!

(Mrs. Elvsted makes a slight gesture of greeting to the other men. Goes to take Hedda's hand. Løvborg rises. He and Mrs. Elvsted greet each other with a silent nod.)

MRS. ELVSTED: Shall I go in and see your husband for a moment?

HEDDA: Oh no, there's no need. Leave them alone; they'll be going out shortly.

MRS. ELVSTED: They're not staying?

HEDDA: No, they're going out to dinner.

MRS. ELVSTED: *(to Løvborg)* Are you going with them?

LØVBORG: No.

HEDDA: Mr. Løvborg will stay with us.

MRS. ELVSTED: *(about to set a chair by his side)* Oh, how nice it is here!

HEDDA: No, Thea, my love. Not there. Come over here by me. I shall sit between you.

MRS. ELVSTED: Just as you please.

(Mrs. Elvsted sits on sofa on Hedda's right. Løvborg reseats himself on his chair.)

LØVBORG: *(after short pause, to Hedda)* Isn't she lovely to look at?

HEDDA: *(stroking her hair)* Only to look at?

LØVBORG: Yes. You see, we are real friends—she and

I. We have absolute trust in each other. We can sit and talk with perfect frankness.

HEDDA: No evasion? Nor circumspection, Mr. Løvborg?

LØVBORG: No—

MRS. ELVSTED: (softly, clinging to Hedda) I'm so very happy, Hedda. Not only this, but he says that I am an inspiration to him, too.

HEDDA: (looks and smiles) Ah! Does he say that?

LØVBORG: And then again, Mrs. Tesman, she is so brave.

MRS. ELVSTED: Brave? Heavens, do you think I'm brave?

LØVBORG: Very—where your friendship with me is concerned.

HEDDA: Yes—courage. If only one had courage!

LØVBORG: And what then? What would it mean?

HEDDA: Then life would be worth living. In spite of everything. (quickly changes the subject) Now, Thea, you must have a glass of cold punch.

MRS. ELVSTED: No, thank you. I never take any.

HEDDA: And you, Mr. Løvborg?

LØVBORG: No, nor I, thank you.

MRS. ELVSTED: No, he never does, either.

HEDDA: (looks straight at him) But if I say you shall?

LØVBORG: It would be no use.

HEDDA: (laughs) Then I have no power over you?

LØVBORG: Not where that is concerned, no.

HEDDA: I think you should—I'm quite serious—for your own sake.

MRS. ELVSTED: Hedda, please!

LØVBORG: What do you mean?

HEDDA: Well, perhaps it's more for other people.

LØVBORG: How so?

HEDDA: Yes. You see, people might very well be suspicious of you...that deep down you really did not trust yourself—that your courage was only skin deep.

MRS. ELVSTED: *(softly)* Oh, please, Hedda.

LØVBORG: People can think what they like—at least for now.

MRS. ELVSTED: *(joyfully)* Yes, yes, let them—

HEDDA: I saw it in Judge Brack a moment ago. It was written all over his face.

LØVBORG: What did you see?

HEDDA: Contempt. In his smile. When you were afraid to join them in there.

LØVBORG: Afraid? The fact is—I chose to stay here and talk with you.

MRS. ELVSTED: There's nothing wrong with that, Hedda.

HEDDA: But the Judge could not know that. In fact, I saw him look at Tesman and smile when you were afraid to join them for their wretched little dinner party.

LØVBORG: You say "afraid" again. Do you think I was afraid?

HEDDA: *I* don't. But that's what Judge Brack thought.

LØVBORG: He can think what he likes.

HEDDA: Then you're not going with them?

LØVBORG: I'm staying here with you and Thea.

MRS. ELVSTED: Hedda, please... you must believe him.

HEDDA: *(smiles and nods her approval)* Strong as a rock! A man of principle—now and forever. Yes, that's how a man should be. *(to Mrs. Elvsted, touching her lightly)* What did I tell you this morning? There was no reason to be so upset.

LØVBORG: What do you mean, "upset"?

MRS. ELVSTED: *(terrified)* Hedda! Oh, Hedda!

HEDDA: You can see for yourself. You were in a state of mortal panic—and there was no need— *(changing the subject)* There—you see. Now we can just enjoy ourselves. The three of us.

LØVBORG: Can you explain yourself, please, Mrs. Tesman?

MRS. ELVSTED: Oh, my God, Hedda... what are you doing? Why...?

HEDDA: Don't get excited. That loathsome Judge Brack is watching you.

LØVBORG: In mortal panic—on my account?

MRS. ELVSTED: *(softly, pitifully)* Oh, Hedda—now you've ruined everything.

LØVBORG: *(Looks at her for a moment. His face is drawn.)* So that was our friendship. That was your trust in me.

MRS. ELVSTED: *(imploringly)* You are my dearest friend— please, let me explain...

LØVBORG: *(takes glass of punch, raises it to his lips, says in husky voice)* Thea, your health! *(empties glass, takes a second)*

MRS. ELVSTED: *(softly)* Hedda, Hedda, how could you do this?

HEDDA: Me? How could I do it? You don't seem to understand.

LØVBORG: And to you, Mrs. Tesman. Your health. Thanks to you for the truth. Here's to truth. *(empties glass and is about to refill it)*

HEDDA: *(lays her hand on his arm)* No more, hmm? That's enough for now. Remember, you're going out to dinner.

MRS. ELVSTED: No. No.

HEDDA: Shhh! They're watching you.

LØVBORG: *(puts glass down)* Now, Thea—tell me the truth.

MRS. ELVSTED: Yes.

LØVBORG: Did your husband know that you had followed me?

MRS. ELVSTED: *(nervous hands)* Oh, Hedda—do you know what he's asking?

LØVBORG: Did he know? Did you arrange to come into town and look after me? Perhaps it was the sheriff's idea? Maybe he needed help at the office, or perhaps he missed me at the card table?

MRS. ELVSTED: *(softly, agonized)* Oh, Løvborg, Løvborg.

LØVBORG: *(about to fill another glass)* Well, here's one for old Sheriff Elvsted.

HEDDA: *(stopping him)* No more just now. You have to read your manuscript to Tesman.

LØVBORG: *(putting down the glass)* Thea, I apologize. There was no reason to take it this way. It was stupid of me. Don't be angry. You are still the dearest of friends. You shall see—you and the others—that if I fell once—that is over. I am on my feet again. Because of you, Thea.

MRS. ELVSTED: *(very happy)* Thank God. Thank God.

(Brack has risen and looked at his watch. He and Tesman enter.)

BRACK: *(takes hat and coat)* Well, Mrs. Tesman, it's time for us to leave.

HEDDA: Yes, I suppose it is.

LØVBORG: *(rising)* For me, too, Judge.

MRS. ELVSTED: *(softly, imploring)* Løvborg, don't go. Don't do it.

HEDDA: *(overlapping, pinching her arm)* They can hear you.

MRS. ELVSTED: *(suppresses a cry of pain)*

LØVBORG: You were kind enough to invite me.

BRACK: So, you're coming after all?

LØVBORG: Yes, if you don't mind.

BRACK: I'd be delighted.

LØVBORG: *(to Tesman, putting manuscript in his overcoat)* I would like to show you one or two things before I send this off to the printers.

TESMAN: Excellent, excellent. That would be delightful. Oh, um, Hedda—how is Mrs. Elvsted to get home?

HEDDA: We'll manage, I'm sure.

LØVBORG: *(looking at the ladies)* Mrs. Elvsted? Oh, of course, I'll come and fetch her. At ten o'clock—or thereabouts. Is that all right, Mrs. Tesman?

HEDDA: Yes, that's perfect. Thank you.

TESMAN: Good. That's settled. I shall probably be home somewhat later, my dear.

HEDDA: You may stay as long as you please.

MRS. ELVSTED: *(concealing her anxiety)* Well then, Mr. Løvborg, I shall wait for you here.

LØVBORG: *(hat in hand)* Please do, Mrs. Elvsted.

BRACK: It's time for the group tour to leave the station. I hope we'll have a "gay old time"—as a certain beautiful lady puts it.

HEDDA: That certain lady would like to be there, but sight unseen.

BRACK: Why unseen?

HEDDA: To listen to all those risqué conversations, Judge.

BRACK: *(laughing)* I would advise the lady against it.

TESMAN: *(also laughing)* Hedda—you ought to be ashamed of yourself.

BRACK: Well, goodbye. We must go. Goodbye.

LØVBORG: *(bowing)* At about ten o'clock, then.

(The men leave. Berte enters inner hall with lighted lamp. Places it on dining room table and leaves.)

MRS. ELVSTED: *(pacing around the room)* Hedda, Hedda, what is going to happen?

HEDDA: At ten o'clock he will be here. I can see him now—in the glow of victory—unafraid. *(smiles)* With vine leaves in his hair.

MRS. ELVSTED: Please, God...

HEDDA: And then, you see—he will be in control once again. He will be a free man once and for all.

MRS. ELVSTED: Oh God, if only he did come back like that—as you see him now.

HEDDA: He will. As I see him. Not any other way. *(goes to her)* You may keep your doubts. *I* believe in him. Now let's try to...

MRS. ELVSTED: What are you hiding from me, Hedda? There's something you want.

HEDDA: Yes, there is. I want—for once in my life—to have power over another human being. To change his destiny.

MRS. ELVSTED: And you haven't that power?

HEDDA: I do not. And I never have.

MRS. ELVSTED: Not over your husband.

HEDDA: That's hardly worth the trouble. You don't understand. Life has made me poor—and you— you are rich. *(takes her in her arms)* Perhaps I should burn off your hair after all.

MRS. ELVSTED: Don't. Please. Stop it. Sometimes you frighten me, Hedda.

BERTE: *(in the doorway)* Tea is ready in the dining room, ma'am.

HEDDA: Thank you. We're coming.

MRS. ELVSTED: No, no. I'd rather go. I'd like to leave right away.

HEDDA: Nonsense. You'll have more tea. Now don't be silly. And then—at ten o'clock—Eilert Løvborg will be here, with vine leaves in his hair.

(she takes Mrs. Elvsted, almost by force, to the doorway)

ACT 3

The same room. The curtains are drawn. A lamp, half turned down, on the table. The stove, door open, has the remains of a fire.

Mrs. Elvsted, wrapped in a large shawl, feet on footrest, sits close to the stove in an armchair. Hedda is asleep on the sofa, covered with a blanket.

Mrs. Elvsted sits up in her chair, listens. Settles back. Speaks softly to herself.

MRS. ELVSTED: Oh, God, God, God. Where is he?

(Berte slips in by hall door, letter in hand)

MRS. ELVSTED: *(turns, whispers)* Has anyone come?

BERTE: *(softly)* Yes. A girl brought this letter.

MRS. ELVSTED: *(holds out hand)* A letter? Give it to me!

BERTE: It's for Dr. Tesman, ma'am.

MRS. ELVSTED: Oh, I see.

BERTE: It was Miss Tesman's girl that brought it. I'll put it on the table.

MRS. ELVSTED: Yes, do.

BERTE: *(putting letter down)* I think I'd better put out the lamp—it's beginning to smoke.

MRS. ELVSTED: Yes, put it out. It will be light soon.

BERTE: *(putting out light)* It's light already, ma'am.

MRS. ELVSTED: Is it? And no one's come back yet?

BERTE: Lord bless you—I knew how it would be.

MRS. ELVSTED: What do you mean?

BERTE: Well, when I saw that a certain person had come back into town—well, when he went out with them. We've heard a lot about that gentleman, I can tell you.

MRS. ELVSTED: Not so loud. You'll wake Mrs. Tesman.

BERTE: *(looks at her, sighs)* No, no. Let her sleep, poor thing. Shall I put some wood on the fire?

MRS. ELVSTED: No, thanks, not for me.

BERTE: Very good, ma'am. *(exits quietly)*

HEDDA: *(awakened by shutting of door)* What's that?

MRS. ELVSTED: That was only the servant.

HEDDA: *(looking about her)* Oh, we're in here! I'd forgotten. *(sits up, stretches)* What time is it?

MRS. ELVSTED: *(looks at watch)* It's past seven.

HEDDA: When did Tesman come home?

MRS. ELVSTED: He didn't.

HEDDA: He's not home yet?

MRS. ELVSTED: *(rising)* No one has come.

HEDDA: And we sat here waiting until four o'clock.

MRS. ELVSTED: *(wringing her hands)* Oh God, I can't get him out of my mind.

HEDDA: *(yawning and covering her mouth with her hand)* We should have saved ourselves the trouble.

MRS. ELVSTED: Were you able to get any sleep?

HEDDA: Oh yes. I slept quite well. And you?

MRS. ELVSTED: I couldn't sleep at all, Hedda. Not for a moment.

HEDDA: *(crosses to her)* There, there. There's nothing to worry about. I know exactly what happened.

MRS. ELVSTED: What? What has happened? Tell me.

HEDDA: Well, of course they kept on drinking at the Judge's—for hours upon hours.

MRS. ELVSTED: Yes. Yes. I'm sure you're right—and then what do you—

HEDDA: So, you see, Tesman didn't like to come home and wake everyone up—ringing the doorbell in the middle of the night. *(laughs)* He probably didn't want anyone to see him either—in the condition he was in.

MRS. ELVSTED: But—where could he have gone?

HEDDA: To his aunt's house, I expect. He must have slept there. They keep his old room ready for him.

MRS. ELVSTED: No, he can't have stayed there. There's a letter for him—from Miss Tesman. It's over there.

HEDDA: Really? *(looks at the address)* Yes. It's from Aunt Julie. Well, he must have spent the night at Judge Brack's. And Eilert Løvborg is there too, with vine leaves in his hair, reading aloud.

MRS. ELVSTED: Hedda, you're just saying that—to make me feel better. You don't really believe it.

HEDDA: You really are a little fool, Thea.

84

MRS. ELVSTED: I'm sorry. I know. I know.

HEDDA: You look so tired.

MRS. ELVSTED: I am. I'm desperately tired.

HEDDA: Then listen to me. Go into my room and lie down on the bed for a while.

MRS. ELVSTED: No, no. I really couldn't sleep.

HEDDA: Of course you can.

MRS. ELVSTED: But your husband will be home soon, I'm sure. And when he does I must know.

HEDDA: I'll tell you as soon as he comes in.

MRS. ELVSTED: You promise?

HEDDA: I promise. Now go and get some sleep.

MRS. ELVSTED: Thank you. I'll try. *(goes to back room)*

(Hedda goes to glass doors, opens the curtains. Broad daylight. Takes hand mirror, arranges her hair. Goes to hall door, rings bell. Berte appears.)

BERTE: Yes, ma'am.

HEDDA: Put some more wood on the stove. I'm freezing.

BERTE: It will warm up in a minute. *(puts log on, stands listening)* That was the doorbell, wasn't it, ma'am?

HEDDA: Well, go and answer it. I'll do the fire.

BERTE: It will soon get going. *(leaves)*

(Hedda kneels, puts log on fire. Tesman enters, tired, serious. Tiptoes to doorway. About to slip in through curtains.)

HEDDA: *(at stove, does not look up)* Good morning.

TESMAN: *(turns)* Hedda! *(going to her)* Good heavens, you're up early!

HEDDA: Yes. I am.

TESMAN: I was sure you'd be still asleep. Fancy that, hmm? Hedda?

HEDDA: Don't talk so loud. Mrs. Elvsted is resting in my room.

TESMAN: Has she been here all night?

HEDDA: Yes. You see, no one came to fetch her.

TESMAN: Yes. Yes, of course.

HEDDA: *(closes stove, rises)* Well—did you enjoy yourselves at Judge Brack's?

TESMAN: Were you worried about me, hmm?

HEDDA: No. That wouldn't have occurred to me. I asked if you enjoyed yourself.

TESMAN: Yes—I did—in a way. Particularly at the beginning of the evening, when Eilert read me part of his book. We were at least an hour too early for dinner, if you can imagine that. Anyway, Brack had a few arrangements to make and so Eilert read to me.

HEDDA: *(seated by the table)* Well—what do you have to tell me...?

TESMAN: *(sitting on footstool near stove)* Oh, Hedda—you can't imagine what that book is going to be like. It is—and I believe this totally—one of the most extraordinary things that has ever been written. Just think!

HEDDA: Yes. Yes, but I don't care about that....

TESMAN: I have to admit—confess, even—that

86

when he had finished reading an awful feeling came over me.

HEDDA: Awful? What do you mean?

TESMAN: I felt jealous. That this man was capable of writing such a profound book. Just think, Hedda.

HEDDA: Oh, I am. I am thinking.

TESMAN: It makes it all the more painful that—with all his gifts—he is nonetheless beyond saving.

HEDDA: You mean that he has more courage than the rest of you?

TESMAN: No, that's not it at all. I mean that he is incapable of any restraint—any control.

HEDDA: Then what happened? In the end?

TESMAN: Well, to be blunt about it—I think it can only be described as debauched.

HEDDA: Were there vine leaves in his hair?

TESMAN: What? Vine leaves? No, I saw nothing of the kind. He made a long, rambling speech—in honor of the woman who had "inspired him in his work." That was his exact phrase.

HEDDA: Did he say who she was?

TESMAN: No. He didn't. But I couldn't help thinking it was Mrs. Elvsted. You can be sure of that.

HEDDA: Well—where was he when you left him?

TESMAN: On his way back to town. We left the party together—those of us who were still there. Brack came with us to get a breath of fresh air. And then we decided we had better take Eilert home. He'd had far more than was good for him.

HEDDA: So I gather.

TESMAN: But now comes the strange part of it, Hedda—sad would be a better word. I am almost ashamed to tell you—for Løvborg's sake—

HEDDA: Go on.

TESMAN: Well, as we were getting closer to town, I fell behind the others a little. Just for a minute or two...I don't know....

HEDDA: Yes? Yes—and then?

TESMAN: And then as I tried to catch up—what do you think I saw lying by the side of the road?

HEDDA: How could I—what did you find?

TESMAN: You mustn't tell a soul, Hedda. Never. You give me your word. For Løvborg's sake. *(takes packet, wrapped in paper, from his pocket)* This. This is what I found. Fancy that.

HEDDA: Isn't that what he had with him yesterday?

TESMAN: Yes. This is the manuscript. All of it. It's irreplaceable. And he just dropped it. And didn't notice. Just think, Hedda—so utterly careless....

HEDDA: *(interrupting)* But why didn't you give it back to him at once?

TESMAN: I couldn't. Not in the state he was in.

HEDDA: Did you tell any of the others that you had found it?

TESMAN: No, of course not. You must understand, surely—for Løvborg's sake. I couldn't do that to him.

HEDDA: So no one knows that you have the manuscript.

88

TESMAN: No. And that's the way it must be.

HEDDA: Then what did you say to him afterward?

TESMAN: I didn't speak to him again. When we actually got into town, he and two or three others just disappeared—gave us the slip, as a matter of fact—if you can imagine.

HEDDA: I see. They must have taken him home, then.

TESMAN: I would think so. Brack went home, too.

HEDDA: And where have you been since then?

TESMAN: I went home with one of the other guests— delightful man—and had morning coffee with him. Or should I say late-night coffee, hmm? But I'm going to take a little rest. And later, when Løvborg has had a chance to sleep it off, I shall take this back to him.

HEDDA: *(holds out hand for package)* No, don't give it to him. Not yet. There's no hurry. Let me read it first.

TESMAN: No, my darling, I can't. I really can't do that.

HEDDA: Why not?

TESMAN: No. Just think how he'll feel when he wakes up. And no manuscript. He'll be absolutely distraught. There is no other copy. He told me.

HEDDA: *(looking at him carefully)* Can it not be reproduced? Written over again?

TESMAN: No, I'm sure that would not be possible. It's a question of inspiration, quite frankly.

HEDDA: Yes. Yes, I suppose it does depend on that. *(lightly)* Oh, by the way, there's a letter for you.

TESMAN: Oh, good heavens.

HEDDA: *(handing it to him)* It came early this morning.

TESMAN: It's from Aunt Julie. What can be the matter? *(puts packet on footstool and opens letter, reads)* Hedda! Oh, Hedda—she says that Aunt Rina is dying.

HEDDA: Well, we were expecting that.

TESMAN: She says that if I want to see her again, I had better hurry. I'll run over there right away.

HEDDA: *(suppressing a smile)* You'll run?

TESMAN: Oh, Hedda—please, my love—would you come with me? If only you could...

HEDDA: *(Rises, tired. Rejects the idea.)* No. Please don't ask me to. I can't bear to be near the presence of sickness and death. I can't. I hate it—the ugliness of it all.

TESMAN: Very well, then, um— *(bustling around)* My hat—coat...it must be in the hall. I hope I shall be in time, Hedda, hmm?

HEDDA: Perhaps if you were to run...

(Berte appears at door)

BERTE: Judge Brack is here. He wants to know if he can come in.

TESMAN: Right now? No, I can't possibly see him.

HEDDA: I can. Ask him to come in.

(Berte leaves)

HEDDA: *(quickly whispering)* The manuscript... *(she picks it up)*

TESMAN: Yes. Give it to me.

HEDDA: No. No, I'll keep it until you come back. *(she places it in the bookcase)*

(Tesman, standing, but in a hurry, cannot get his gloves on. Judge Brack enters.)

HEDDA: *(nods a greeting)* You're up with the dawn, I must say.

BRACK: Yes. Aren't I? *(to Tesman)* You're on your way out?

TESMAN: Yes, I must rush off to Aunt Rina. She's very weak. I'm sorry to say she won't survive this time.

BRACK: Oh dear, I'm sorry to hear it. Then, please, don't let me detain you—at such a difficult time.

TESMAN: Yes, I must rush off. Goodbye, then— goodbye. *(exits)*

HEDDA: *(approaching him)* Well, Judge Brack, it seems you made quite a night of it.

BRACK: I can assure you, dear Mrs. Tesman, that I did not get undressed.

HEDDA: Ah. You, too?

BRACK: As you can see. But did Tesman tell you about our adventures last night?

HEDDA: Oh yes, he bored me with the details—he had coffee somewhere or other.

BRACK: Yes, I've heard about that already. Eilert Løvborg was not with them?

91

HEDDA: No—they'd taken him home some time before that.

BRACK: Was Tesman with them?

HEDDA: No. It was some of the others, I gather.

BRACK: Jørgen Tesman is such an innocent. *(smiles)* Really he is.

HEDDA: Yes. *(looking at him)* That he is. Then there was something else?

BRACK: I think perhaps there was.

HEDDA: Please sit down, my dear Judge. Make yourself comfortable. And tell me what happened. *(She sits at left of table. Brack sits near her on long side of table.)*

HEDDA: Now, then?

BRACK: I had particular reasons for keeping track of my guests last night—at least some of my guests.

HEDDA: Eilert Løvborg in particular, perhaps?

BRACK: Frankly, yes.

HEDDA: That's very interesting. Please go on.

BRACK: Do you know where he—and one or two of the others—ended up last night?

HEDDA: If it's not somewhere unmentionable, then tell me.

BRACK: Oh no, it's not at all like that. Well, they put in an appearance at a particularly lively party.

HEDDA: Just lively, or could you call it a wild party?

BRACK: That would be accurate, I think.

HEDDA: Go on. Tell me more.

BRACK: Løvborg, and, indeed, some of the others, had been invited beforehand. I knew all about it. But, of course, he had declined; since, as you know, he has become a new man.

HEDDA: At the Elvsteds, yes, he has. So he went after all, then?

BRACK: Well, you see, my dear Mrs. Tesman. . . . Unfortunately, when he was at my party—how shall I put it—the spirit moved him . . .

HEDDA: Yes, I heard that he found inspiration.

BRACK: Of a most vehement kind. Well, I expect that changed his mind. We men are not always so strong—so principled—as we ought to be.

HEDDA: You, I'm sure, are an exception, Judge Brack. But Løvborg—what happened—?

BRACK: To make a long story short, he ended up in Mademoiselle Diana's apartment.

HEDDA: Mademoiselle Diana?

BRACK: It was she who was giving the party—to a select circle of her male admirers and female friends.

HEDDA: Does she have auburn hair?

BRACK: She does.

HEDDA: She's an entertainer—a chanteuse?

BRACK: Yes, when she has the time. Actually, she's more of a huntress than a singer. She hunts men. You must have heard of her, Mrs. Tesman. Eilert Løvborg was one of her more enthusiastic admirers—before he became a new man.

HEDDA: What happened in the end?

BRACK: Well, it wasn't very friendly—at least, so I've heard. After a most tender beginning, it seems that they actually came to blows....

HEDDA: She and Løvborg?

BRACK: Yes. He accused her of stealing. He claimed he'd lost a wallet—and one or two other things as well. In short, he seems to have made a rather ugly scene.

HEDDA: So what happened then?

BRACK: I gather that there was a general free-for-all, in which not only the gentlemen but the ladies too took part. Fortunately, the police arrived before it went much further.

HEDDA: The police were there?

BRACK: Yes. I'm sure it will prove an expensive evening for Mr. Løvborg. The man is quite mad.

HEDDA: Why did you say "expensive"?

BRACK: I'm told he was quite violent—he struck a policeman in the face and tore the coat off his back. So he was taken into custody, along with the others.

HEDDA: How did you find all of this out?

BRACK: From the police. I went down to the station.

HEDDA: *(gazing straight ahead)* So that is what happened. There were no vine leaves in his hair.

BRACK: Vine leaves, Mrs. Tesman?

HEDDA: *(changing tone)* Judge—tell me...why did you—what was the real reason for your tracking him down like that?

BRACK: Well, in the first place, it would be of some

importance to me if—during the course of the trial—it should emerge that Løvborg created this disturbance after leaving a party at my house.

HEDDA: Will it come to trial, then?

BRACK: Of course. However, that is of marginal concern to me. I "tracked him down" because I thought that as a friend of the family, I ought to supply you and Tesman with a full account of his nocturnal adventures.

HEDDA: Why did you think so, Judge Brack?

BRACK: Why? Because I have a shrewd suspicion that he intends to use you both as a sort of front—

HEDDA: Oh, how can you think such a thing?

BRACK: I'm not completely blind, my dear Hedda. Mark my words. Mrs. Elvsted will not be going home for some time.

HEDDA: Well, even if there *is* something between them, I should think there are plenty of other places where they could meet.

BRACK: Perhaps, but not a single home. It will be as it was before. Every respectable house will be closed to Eilert Løvborg.

HEDDA: As should mine, you mean?

BRACK: Yes. I must confess that it would be painful for me if this—this person were given free access to your home. He would be out of place—an intruder, even—if he managed to force his way into—

HEDDA: Into our little *ménage à trois*.

BRACK: Precisely. It would mean, quite simply, that I should find myself without a home.

HEDDA: *(smiles)* You want to be the one cock of the walk—that is what you want, hmm?

BRACK: *(nods and lowers his voice)* Yes, that is what I want. And I shall fight for it—with every weapon I can find.

HEDDA: *(smile fades)* You can be a dangerous man, Judge Brack—when the need arises.

BRACK: Do you think so?

HEDDA: I'm beginning to. In fact, I feel quite relieved that—you have no hold over me.

BRACK: *(with an ambiguous laugh)* Well, Mrs. Tesman, perhaps you're right to feel that way. Otherwise, who knows what I might be capable of?

HEDDA: That sounds like a threat.

BRACK: Oh, no, not at all. If our ménage is to exist, it must be unforced—spontaneous.

HEDDA: There I agree with you.

BRACK: Well, I have said all that I had to say. I should be getting back to town. Goodbye, Mrs. Tesman. *(going to glass door)*

HEDDA: Are you going through the garden?

BRACK: Yes, it's quicker.

HEDDA: And, of course, it's the back way.

BRACK: Exactly. I have no objections to that. In fact, it can be an exhilarating place to be.

HEDDA: During target practice, you mean?

BRACK: *(in doorway, laughing)* Ah, but people don't shoot their tame poultry.

HEDDA: *(also laughing)* No. Not when there's only one cock of the walk.

(They nod goodbye. He goes. She closes the door.)

(Hedda is serious. Stands, looks out, then goes to look through curtain of middle doorway. Takes Løvborg's package out of bookcase. Starts to look at it. Berte is heard, speaking loudly, in the doorway. Hedda turns, listens. Locks package in drawer, puts key on inkstand. Løvborg, with greatcoat and hat in hand, rushes in, confused, irritated.)

LØVBORG: *(turning back)* I must and I will come in. *(closes door, sees Hedda, gains control, bows)*

HEDDA: *(at writing table)* Well, Mr. Løvborg, isn't it rather late—to be calling for Thea?

LØVBORG: On the contrary. It's rather early to be calling on you. Please forgive me.

HEDDA: How do you know she is still here?

LØVBORG: They told me at her lodgings that she had not yet come home.

HEDDA: *(going to oval table)* And when they told you that, did you notice anything—anything strange?

LØVBORG: *(looking at her)* What do you mean, "strange"?

HEDDA: I mean, did they seem to think it odd?

LØVBORG: *(finally understanding)* Ah yes, of course. I'm dragging her down with me. No, in fact, I didn't notice anything. I suppose Tesman is not yet up?

HEDDA: No. I don't think so.

LØVBORG: When did he come home?

HEDDA: Very late.

97

LØVBORG: Did he say anything?

HEDDA: Yes. I gather you had a particularly lively evening at Judge Brack's.

LØVBORG: Is that all?

HEDDA: There was more, I believe—but I was so dreadfully sleepy.

(Mrs. Elvsted enters)

MRS. ELVSTED: *(going to him)* Ah, Løvborg—at last.

LØVBORG: Yes—at last. And too late.

MRS. ELVSTED: *(looking at him)* Why too late?

LØVBORG: It's too late for everything now. It's all over.

MRS. ELVSTED: No. No. Don't say that.

LØVBORG: That is what you will say, too, when I tell you...

MRS. ELVSTED: Then I don't *want* to hear. Nothing!

HEDDA: Perhaps you would like to speak to her alone—? I'll leave you.

LØVBORG: *(rudely)* No, stay—you too. Please. Please stay.

MRS. ELVSTED: I will *not* listen. Not to anything.

LØVBORG: I don't want to talk about what happened last night. It's not that.

MRS. ELVSTED: What, then?

LØVBORG: I've come to tell you that we must not see each other again.

MRS. ELVSTED: But why?

HEDDA: *(involuntarily—to self)* I knew it.

LØVBORG: You can be of no more service to me, Thea.

MRS. ELVSTED: How can you stand there and say that! No more service! Look, I can help you now—still—as I did before. We can work together. I know we can.

LØVBORG: I have no more work to do.

MRS. ELVSTED: *(in despair)* Then what am I to do with my life?

LØVBORG: You must go on as before—as if you'd never met me.

MRS. ELVSTED: I can't. You know I can't.

LØVBORG: You must try, Thea. You must go back home again.

MRS. ELVSTED: *(angry, protesting)* Never. Never. Not in this life. Wherever you are, there I will be also. I will not be driven out like this. I will be with you when the book is published.

HEDDA: *(half-whisper, in suspense)* Yes—the book.

LØVBORG: Yes—my book and Thea's. For that is what it is.

MRS. ELVSTED: I believe that. I feel it. And that is why I have a right to be with you when it is published. I want to see you glowing, once again, with pride and self-respect. And the happiness—oh, the happiness—I must share that with you.

LØVBORG: Thea, our book will never be published.

HEDDA: Ah.

MRS. ELVSTED: Never be published...

LØVBORG: No. Never.

MRS. ELVSTED: *(agonized, fearing the worst)* Løvborg— what have you done with the manuscript?

HEDDA: *(looks anxiously at him)* Yes—the manuscript...

MRS. ELVSTED: Where is it?

LØVBORG: Thea—don't ask me about it.

MRS. ELVSTED: Yes. Yes, I must know. I demand to know. Now.

LØVBORG: The manuscript—yes. Well, if—I have torn it into a thousand pieces.

MRS. ELVSTED: *(shrieks)* No! No!

HEDDA: *(involuntarily)* But that's not true.

LØVBORG: *(looks at her)* Not true, do you think?

HEDDA: *(collecting herself)* I—well, if you say so. It sounded so improbable.

LØVBORG: It's true, all the same.

MRS. ELVSTED: *(wringing her hands)* Oh, God, God. Hedda—he's torn his own work to pieces.

LØVBORG: My life is in pieces. Why not my work?

MRS. ELVSTED: When? Last night?

LØVBORG: Yes. I've told you. I tore it into a thousand pieces. And I scattered them on the waters of the fjord—far out where the water is sea-cold. Let them drift upon it—drift with the current and the wind. Soon they will sink—deep—then deeper and deeper, as I shall sink, Thea.

MRS. ELVSTED: You don't know what you've done. Do you know how I feel—how I shall feel to my dying day? It is as if you had killed a newborn child.

LØVBORG: I understand. It *is* like the death of a child.

MRS. ELVSTED: How could you? It was mine, too.

HEDDA: *(almost inaudibly)* The child—

MRS. ELVSTED: *(breathing heavily)* Then it is finished. Well, I will go now, Hedda.

HEDDA: Will you leave town?

MRS. ELVSTED: I don't know what I shall do. I see nothing. Nothing but darkness. *(exits by hall door)*

HEDDA: *(stands waiting)* Are you not going to see her home, Mr. Løvborg?

LØVBORG: I? Through the streets? In broad daylight? With people staring at us walking together? Is that what you suggest?

HEDDA: Of course, I don't know what else happened last night. But is the situation so irretrievable?

LØVBORG: Last night was just the beginning of the end. I know that. And the strange thing is that that sort of life has no appeal for me now. But she has broken my courage. I have no strength left for life.

HEDDA: *(looking straight ahead)* That simple, pretty nothing of a woman has changed a man's destiny. *(looking at him)* But how could you treat her so cruelly?

LØVBORG: Don't say that it was cruel.

HEDDA: You destroyed something that had lived in her soul for months. That wasn't cruel?

LØVBORG: Hedda, I can tell the truth to you.

HEDDA: The truth?

LØVBORG: First, you must promise, you must give me your word, that Thea will never know what I am about to tell you.

HEDDA: I give you my word.

LØVBORG: So. In the first place, what I said just now is untrue.

HEDDA: About the manuscript?

LØVBORG: Yes. I did not tear it to pieces. I did not throw it into the fjord.

HEDDA: Then—but where is it?

LØVBORG: I have destroyed it all the same—totally destroyed it, Hedda.

HEDDA: I don't understand.

LØVBORG: Thea said that what I had done was like killing a child.

HEDDA: Yes.

LØVBORG: But for a man to kill his child is—that is not the worst thing he can do to it.

HEDDA: Not the worst?

LØVBORG: No. I wanted to spare Thea from hearing that.

HEDDA: Then what is the worst?

LØVBORG: Let us think of a man who comes home, in the early hours of the morning, comes home to the mother of his child—he's been drinking heavily, the night was a debauch, and he says to her: "Listen—I've been out all night, here, there and everywhere.... Look, I took the child with me—and he's lost. Completely lost. God knows where he is—God knows who may have their hands on him."

HEDDA: Yes, but after all, this was not a child—it was only a book, a manuscript.

LØVBORG: But Thea's soul was in that book.

HEDDA: Yes, I understand.

LØVBORG: Then you can understand that there is no future for us together.

HEDDA: Then where will you go from here?

LØVBORG: Nowhere. I will try to make an end of it all—as quickly as possible.

HEDDA: *(moving closer)* Eilert Løvborg, I want you to listen to me. When the time comes... will you not do it beautifully?

LØVBORG: Beautifully. *(smiles at her)* With vine leaves in my hair? That was your fantasy—a long time ago.

HEDDA: No. No. No more. The vine leaves have withered. But beautifully, nevertheless. For once. ... You must go now. Goodbye. You must never come here again.

LØVBORG: Goodbye, Mrs. Tesman. Give Jørgen Tesman my love. *(he starts to leave)*

HEDDA: Wait. I want to give you something to take with you—a memento. *(Goes to drawer, takes out pistol case. Returns to Løvborg with one of the pistols.)*

LØVBORG: *(looks at her)* This—is this the memento?

HEDDA: *(nodding slowly)* Do you recognize it? It was aimed at you once.

LØVBORG: You should have used it then.

HEDDA: Take it—it's for you to use now.

LØVBORG: *(puts pistol in breast pocket)* I thank you.

HEDDA: Beautifully, Eilert Løvborg. Promise me that.

LØVBORG: Goodbye, Hedda Gabler. *(exits)*

(Hedda listens for a while. Goes to drawer, takes out manuscript. Takes out a few sheets. Looks at them. Sits in armchair by stove, package in her lap. Opens the stove, after a while, then unwraps whole package.)

HEDDA: *(throws a sheaf into the stove and whispers)* Thea, Thea, I am burning your child. It burns. Hair on fire. *(throws more on)* Your child and Eilert Løvborg's child. *(throws rest in)* It burns—I am burning your child.

ACT 4

The same day. It is evening. In darkness. The back room is lit by a hanging lamp. The curtains over the glass door are closed. Hedda, dressed in black, walks about the room. She goes to the back room and disappears for a moment. A few chords are heard on the piano. Then she returns.

Berte enters from the inner room. She places a lighted lamp on the table in front of the corner settee. Her eyes are red with weeping. Black ribbons in her cap. She exits quietly. Hedda goes to the curtains and looks into the darkness.

Miss Tesman enters in mourning, with bonnet and veil. Hedda goes to her, holding out her hands.

MISS TESMAN: Yes, Hedda, here I am—in my grief. I'm alone now. My poor sister has found peace at last.

HEDDA: I had heard—as you can see. Tesman sent word.

MISS TESMAN: Yes, he promised he would. But all the same I felt I had to come myself. To bring the news of death to this house of life.

HEDDA: That was most kind of you.

MISS TESMAN: She shouldn't have left us now. This is not the time for Hedda's house to be a house of mourning.

HEDDA: *(changing the subject)* She died quite peacefully, I gather, Miss Tesman?

MISS TESMAN: Oh, the end was so calm, so...so beautiful. And she was able to see Jørgen for the last time—she was able to say goodbye to him. I know that made her very happy. Content. Has he not come home yet?

HEDDA: No. He said in the note that he might be detained. Won't you sit down?

MISS TESMAN: No, thank you, my dear, dear Hedda. I would like to—but I have so much to do. I must prepare my dear sister for her eternal sleep. She shall go to her grave looking her best.

HEDDA: Can I be of any help?

MISS TESMAN: Oh, I wouldn't think of it. Hedda Tesman must have nothing to do with the sadness of death. And she must not even think about it, either—not at this time.

HEDDA: One is not always mistress of one's own thoughts....

MISS TESMAN: *(continuing)* That is the way of the world. At home we shall be sewing the shroud; and here they'll be sewing other things—and soon, too, thank God.

(Tesman enters)

HEDDA: Ah, you've come home at last.

TESMAN: You here, Aunt Julie? And with Hedda? Fancy that.

MISS TESMAN: I was just going, my dear boy. Well, have you done all that you promised?

TESMAN: No. I'm sorry. I'm afraid I forgot half

of it. I'll come to see you tomorrow. My brain is spinning today—can't keep my thoughts straight.

MISS TESMAN: Oh, Jørgen, my dear, dear Jørgen. You mustn't take it like this.

TESMAN: How? What do you mean?

MISS TESMAN: Even in your grief you must find happiness. You must be happy that she is at rest.

TESMAN: Oh, yes, yes, you're thinking of Aunt Rina.

HEDDA: You will feel lonely now, Miss Tesman.

MISS TESMAN: I expect so. At first. But that won't last too long, I hope. One must go on. I'm sure I'll find someone to take poor Rina's little room.

TESMAN: Really? Who do you think will take it?

MISS TESMAN: Oh, there's always someone who needs looking after, isn't there? Unfortunately.

HEDDA: Would you really take all that on yourself once again?

MISS TESMAN: All that! Heaven forgive you, child— it was no trouble at all for me.

HEDDA: But a complete stranger—how would you—

MISS TESMAN: One soon makes friends—particularly when someone is not well and needs you. I have to have someone to live for. I have to. But perhaps there'll soon be something to keep an old aunt busy in this house. And I thank heaven for it.

HEDDA: Don't worry about anything here.

TESMAN: Yes, just think what a wonderful time we three could have if—

HEDDA: If?

TESMAN: *(uneasily)* Oh, nothing. Everything will be fine. Let's hope so, hmm?

MISS TESMAN: Well, I'm sure you two want to talk to each other. *(smiling)* And perhaps Hedda has something special to tell you, Jørgen. So, good-bye. I must go home to Rina. *(stops at door)* To Rina. Isn't it strange? She's with me still, and with my poor brother as well.

TESMAN: Yes, just think of that, Aunt Julie. Yes.

(Miss Tesman leaves)

HEDDA: *(looks coldly at Tesman)* I almost believe you are more upset at Aunt Rina's death than Aunt Julie is.

TESMAN: It's not only that. I am very worried about Eilert Løvborg.

HEDDA: *(quickly)* Is there any news?

TESMAN: I went to his rooms this afternoon. I wanted to tell him that his manuscript was safe.

HEDDA: Well, did you see him?

TESMAN: No. He wasn't in. But afterward I met Mrs. Elvsted. And she told me he had been here early this morning.

HEDDA: Yes. As soon as you'd left.

TESMAN: He said that he'd torn his manuscript to pieces?

HEDDA: Yes—that's what he said.

TESMAN: God! He must have been completely out his mind. I suppose you thought it best not to give it back to him?

HEDDA: He did not get it.

TESMAN: But of course you told him that we had it.

HEDDA: No. *(quickly)* Did you tell Mrs. Elvsted?

TESMAN: No. I thought it better not to. But you should have told him, Hedda. Just think. He must be absolutely distraught. What if he should do himself some harm? Give me the manuscript, Hedda. I shall take it to him right away. Where is it?

HEDDA: *(cold, unmoved, leaning on armchair)* I have not got it.

TESMAN: Have not got it? What are you talking about?

HEDDA: I have burnt it—every single word of it.

TESMAN: *(horrified)* Burnt it! Burnt Eilert's manuscript!

HEDDA: Don't shout. The servant will hear you.

TESMAN: Burnt it. Good God.... No. No. That's impossible.

HEDDA: It is true, nevertheless.

TESMAN: Do you understand what you've done, Hedda? Apart from everything else, it was stolen. Stolen. Do you understand? Judge Brack will tell you what that means.

HEDDA: I think it would be wise not to speak of it again—neither to Judge Brack nor to anyone else.

TESMAN: It's unheard of—how could you do such a thing? What got into you? What made you think of it? Answer me that...

HEDDA: *(almost imperceptible smile)* I did it for your sake, Jørgen.

TESMAN: For me?!

HEDDA: This morning—what you told me about what he had read to you—

TESMAN: Yes, yes—what then?

HEDDA: You admitted that you had feelings of jealousy.

TESMAN: Yes, but that was natural. I didn't mean anything by it.

HEDDA: No matter. I couldn't bear the idea of you living in someone else's shadow.

TESMAN: *(half doubting, half overjoyed)* Oh, Hedda, Hedda. Is this true? But you...you've never shown your love to me like that. Never.

HEDDA: Well, I may as well tell you...at this time— at this time—I'm...*(breaks off)* No. No. You can ask Aunt Julie. She will tell you soon enough.

TESMAN: I think I understand. Hedda...is it true? Oh, Hedda!

HEDDA: Quiet. The servant will hear.

TESMAN: *(laughing)* The servant. Oh, Hedda, don't be so absurd. It's only Berte. I'll tell her myself.

HEDDA: *(hands knotted in desperation)* This is killing me—killing me, all this.

TESMAN: What? What is it, Hedda?

HEDDA: *(cold, in control)* All this—this absurdity. *(spelling it out)* This absurdity, Jørgen.

TESMAN: This absurdity! That I'm so happy at the news! What's absurd about that? But I won't say anything. I won't say anything to Berte.

HEDDA: Oh, why not that, too?

TESMAN: No. No, not yet. But I must tell Aunt Julie. Did you realize that you called me Jørgen a moment ago? Oh, Hedda, Aunt Julie will be so happy.

HEDDA: When she learns that I have burnt Eilert Løvborg's manuscript—for your sake?

TESMAN: That's not—look, as for the manuscript, of course no one must know about that. I'm talking about a different fire—your love for me. That is what I must share with Aunt Julie. I wonder, does this often happen when a marriage is so young?

HEDDA: Perhaps you should ask Aunt Julie that question, too.

TESMAN: I will—sometime soon, I will. *(looks weary and worried again)* But the manuscript—it . . . The manuscript! Good God, it's terrible to think of what will happen to Eilert now.

(Mrs. Elvsted, dressed as in Act 1, enters by hall door)

MRS. ELVSTED: *(greets them hurriedly, evidently agitated)* My dear Hedda, please forgive my coming back.

HEDDA: What is the matter with you, Thea?

TESMAN: Is it Eilert Løvborg again?

MRS. ELVSTED: Yes. I'm very afraid that something awful has happened to him.

HEDDA: *(taking her arm)* Do you think so?

TESMAN: Good Lord, Mrs. Elvsted. Why do you think that?

MRS. ELVSTED: I went back to my boarding house, and I overheard some people talking about him— just as I came in. The stories that are going around—it's hard to believe.

TESMAN: Yes, I've heard a few things, too. But I can swear that he went straight home to bed last night.

HEDDA: Well, what did they say at the boarding house?

MRS. ELVSTED: Well, I didn't really hear anything at all—not clearly. Perhaps they did not know anything definite—or else... In any case, they stopped talking when they saw me, and I didn't have the courage to ask.

TESMAN: *(pacing uneasily)* Well, let's hope, Mrs. Elvsted, let's hope that there was a misunderstanding.

MRS. ELVSTED: No. No. I'm sure that they were talking about him—I'm sure. I think, in fact, that I heard the hospital mentioned—

TESMAN: The hospital?

HEDDA: Surely not!

MRS. ELVSTED: It terrified me. I went to his lodgings and asked for him there.

HEDDA: You actually had the courage to go there?

MRS. ELVSTED: What else could I do? Just not knowing—I couldn't bear that any longer.

TESMAN: But you didn't find him.

MRS. ELVSTED: No. And the people there knew nothing about him. They said he hadn't been home since yesterday afternoon.

TESMAN: Since yesterday—fancy that. But how could they say that?

MRS. ELVSTED: I know something terrible has happened to him. I can feel it.

TESMAN: Hedda, my dear—how would it be if I were to go and make some inquiries...?

HEDDA: No, no, you must not get involved in this.

(Judge Brack, hat in hand, enters through hall door which Berte opens. He looks grave. Bows in silence.)

TESMAN: *(while Judge is in hallway)* Is that you, Judge?

BRACK: Yes. It was imperative that I should see you this evening.

TESMAN: You've heard the news about Aunt Rina?

BRACK: Yes, that among other things.

TESMAN: It's sad, isn't it?

BRACK: Well, my dear Tesman, that depends on how you look at it.

TESMAN: *(looks at him inquiringly)* Has—has anything else happened?

BRACK: Yes.

HEDDA: *(in suspense)* Is it upsetting, Judge Brack?

BRACK: That, too, depends on how you look at it, Mrs. Tesman.

MRS. ELVSTED: *(unable to restrain her anxiety)* It's Eilert Løvborg, isn't it? Something has happened to him.

113

BRACK: *(quick glance at her)* What makes you say that, madam? Have you already heard something?

MRS. ELVSTED: *(in confusion)* No, nothing. I've heard nothing, but...

TESMAN: For God's sake, tell us!

BRACK: *(shrugs shoulders)* Well, I regret to have to tell you that Eilert Løvborg has been taken to the hospital. He is lying on the point of death.

MRS. ELVSTED: *(screams)* Oh, God! Oh, God!

TESMAN: To the hospital! At the point of death.

HEDDA: *(quickly)* So soon.

MRS. ELVSTED: *(wailing)* We parted in anger, Hedda!

HEDDA: *(whispers)* Thea, Thea—be careful.

MRS. ELVSTED: *(ignoring her)* I must go to him—I must see him while he's still alive.

BRACK: It is useless, madam. No one can be admitted.

MRS. ELVSTED: Tell me—please—tell me, what happened to him? What is it?

TESMAN: *(to Brack)* Are you implying that he—that he himself—

HEDDA: Yes. Yes. I'm sure of it.

TESMAN: Hedda—how can you...?

BRACK: *(looking right at her)* Unfortunately, Mrs. Tesman, your guess was quite correct.

MRS. ELVSTED: It's awful—awful—awful—

TESMAN: He did it, then. Himself. Fancy that.

HEDDA: Shot himself.

BRACK: Another correct guess, Mrs. Tesman.

MRS. ELVSTED: *(trying to regain composure)* When did it happen, Mr. Brack?

BRACK: This afternoon, between three and four.

TESMAN: But—oh, my God—where was he? Where did he do it?

BRACK: *(hesitant)* Where—I suppose it must have been at his lodgings—

MRS. ELVSTED: No, that's impossible. I was there between six and seven.

BRACK: Then it must have been somewhere else. I really don't know. All I know is that he found ... he had shot himself—in the heart.

MRS. ELVSTED: Oh, my God—that he should die like that!

HEDDA: *(to Brack)* Was it in the heart?

BRACK: Yes—that's what I said.

HEDDA: Not in the temple?

BRACK: In the heart, Mrs. Tesman.

HEDDA: Well, that too has its beauty.

BRACK: What do you mean, Mrs. Tesman?

HEDDA: Oh, nothing. Nothing.

TESMAN: And the wound is—is critical, you say.

BRACK: Absolutely mortal. The end has probably come by this time.

MRS. ELVSTED: Yes, I know it—I know it. The end ... Oh, Hedda!

TESMAN: How did you learn all of this?

BRACK: *(quickly)* From one of the police. A man I had dealt with before.

HEDDA: *(in a clear voice)* At last an act that has some meaning.

TESMAN: *(terrified)* Good God, Hedda, what are you saying?

HEDDA: I mean that there is beauty in this act.

BRACK: Ah, Mrs. Tesman—

TESMAN: Beauty! How can—

MRS. ELVSTED: Oh, Hedda, where in God's name is the beauty?

HEDDA: Eilert Løvborg has settled his account with life. He made a choice. He had the courage to do it—to do the one thing that had to be done.

MRS. ELVSTED: No, that is not how it happened. You can't think that. It was beyond reason. He must have been out of control.

TESMAN: Utterly distraught.

HEDDA: I do not believe that. He chose—

MRS. ELVSTED: No. He was out of his mind. Just as he was when he tore up his manuscript.

BRACK: The manuscript? Did he tear it up?

MRS. ELVSTED: Yes. Last night.

TESMAN: *(whispers)* Oh, Hedda, we shall never get over this.

BRACK: That's quite extraordinary.

TESMAN: *(pacing)* I can't accept the idea of Løvborg's—of him taking leave of this life. And then not to leave behind him the book that would have made his name immortal—

116

MRS. ELVSTED: Oh, if only it could be put together again.

TESMAN: Yes. Yes, if only it could. I would give anything—anything.

MRS. ELVSTED: Perhaps it can, Mr. Tesman.

TESMAN: What do you mean?

MRS. ELVSTED: *(searches in the pocket of her dress)* Look at these. I kept them. These are his notes—he would write down his ideas and then dictate to me.

HEDDA: *(stepping forward)* Ah—

TESMAN: And you kept them—all of them?

MRS. ELVSTED: Yes, they're all here. I brought them with me when I—when I left home. They're all here.

TESMAN: Let me see them.

MRS. ELVSTED: *(handing the bundle of papers)* They're in no particular order, I'm afraid—all mixed up.

TESMAN: But just think if we could make something out of them! Perhaps if the two of us worked on it together.

MRS. ELVSTED: Yes. Oh, yes. We have to at least try.

TESMAN: We shall do more than that—we shall do it. For me there will be nothing else but that. That will be my life.

HEDDA: You, Jørgen? Your life?

TESMAN: Yes. Every moment that I can spare. My own research must wait. Hedda—you understand, don't you? I owe this to Eilert Løvborg. I owe it to his memory.

HEDDA: Perhaps.

TESMAN: And so, my dear Mrs. Elvsted, that is what we shall do. We shall give our minds to it. Totally. There is no use in brooding over what can never be changed. We must try to control our grief—as far as that is possible—and...

MRS. ELVSTED: Yes. Yes, Mr. Tesman. I will do the best I can.

TESMAN: Well, then, be good enough to come with me. I can't wait to begin. We must look through the notes together. But I don't think we should sit in here. No. Let's go in there—into the back room. Excuse me, my dear Judge. Come with me, Mrs. Elvsted.

MRS. ELVSTED: Oh, if only it were possible.

(They go into the back room. Mrs. Elvsted takes off her cloak and hat. They sit at the table under the hanging lamp and begin an eager examination of the papers. Hedda crosses to the stove and sits in the armchair. Brack goes to her.)

HEDDA: *(in a low voice)* Oh, what a feeling of freedom it gives one—this act of Eilert Løvborg's.

BRACK: Freedom, Mrs. Tesman? Well, of course, it is a release for him.

HEDDA: I mean for me. It gives me a sense of freedom to know that an act of deliberate courage is still possible in this world—an act that was both spontaneous and beautiful.

BRACK: *(smiling)* My dear Mrs. Tesman...

HEDDA: Oh, I know what you're going to say. You, too, are a specialist. You, too—like...

BRACK: *(looking at her)* Perhaps Eilert Løvborg meant

more to you than you are willing to admit. Am I wrong?

HEDDA: I do not answer such questions. All I know is that Eilert Løvborg had the courage to live his life as he chose. And then the last, great act—an act of beauty. He had the will, he had the strength to turn away from the banquet of life—so early.

BRACK: I am sorry, Mrs. Tesman, but I'm afraid I must shatter that comfortable illusion.

HEDDA: Illusion?

BRACK: Yes—which could not have lasted very long in any case.

HEDDA: What do you mean?

BRACK: Eilert Løvborg did shoot himself—but it was not a matter of choice.

HEDDA: Not a matter of choice?

BRACK: No. It did not happen in quite the same way as I described.

HEDDA: *(in suspense)* You were hiding something. What was it?

BRACK: Well, for poor Mrs. Elvsted's sake, I ... idealized the facts somewhat.

HEDDA: What are the facts?

BRACK: First, Løvborg is already dead.

HEDDA: At the hospital?

BRACK: Yes—without gaining consciousness.

HEDDA: And what else have you kept hidden?

BRACK: It did not happen at his lodgings.

HEDDA: That makes no difference.

BRACK: Perhaps. But I have to tell you that Løvborg was found shot—in...in Mademoiselle Diana's boudoir.

HEDDA: *(makes a half attempt to rise)* That's impossible. He can't have been there again today.

BRACK: He was there this afternoon. He went there—so I understand—to demand the return of something that they had taken from him. He talked, somewhat wildly, about a child—a lost child—

HEDDA: Oh...then that was why.

BRACK: I felt sure he meant his manuscript, but now I gather he destroyed it himself. I suppose it must have been his wallet.

HEDDA: Yes. I suppose so. And it was there that he was found.

BRACK: Yes. With a pistol in his breast pocket—it had been fired. And the bullet had passed through his chest and lodged in a vital part.

HEDDA: In the heart—

BRACK: No—in the bowels.

HEDDA: *(looks at him with an expression of loathing)* That too. Oh, what is it that makes everything I touch turn ugly and mean?

BRACK: There is one last thing, Mrs. Tesman—one last unpleasant feature.

HEDDA: And what is that?

BRACK: This pistol that he had—

HEDDA: *(breathless)* Well, what about it?

BRACK: He must have stolen it.

HEDDA: *(leaps up)* Stolen it! That is simply not true. He did not steal it.

BRACK: No other explanation is possible. He must have stolen it. Shh!

(Tesman and Mrs. Elvsted have risen from the table and entered the drawing room)

TESMAN: *(papers in both hands)* Hedda, my dear, it's almost impossible to read under that lamp—just think.

HEDDA: I am. I am thinking.

TESMAN: Would you mind if we sat at your writing table?

HEDDA: If you like. *(quickly)* No, wait. Let me clear it first.

TESMAN: Oh, don't bother. There's plenty of room.

HEDDA: No. Let me clear it. Please! I'll take these things and put them on the piano. There.

(She has taken something, covered with sheet music, from under the bookcase. She puts more music sheets upon it, takes it into the other room. Tesman lays the scraps of paper on the writing table and moves the lamp from the corner table. He and Mrs. Elvsted sit down and get on with their work. Hedda returns.)

HEDDA: *(behind Mrs. Elvsted's chair, gently ruffling her hair)* Well, my lovely Thea, how is it? How is this memorial to Eilert Løvborg?

MRS. ELVSTED: *(looking at her)* Oh, it will be dreadfully difficult to put it in order.

TESMAN: But we must do it. I am determined.

Besides, it's something I'm good at—working on other people's papers, setting them in order.

(Hedda goes to the stove, sits. Brack stands over her.)

HEDDA: *(whispers)* What did you say about the pistol?

BRACK: *(softly)* That he must have stolen it.

HEDDA: Why stolen it?

BRACK: Because every other explanation ought to be unthinkable, Mrs. Tesman.

HEDDA: Indeed?

BRACK: *(glares at her)* Of course, Eilert Løvborg was here this morning, wasn't he?

HEDDA: Yes.

BRACK: Were you alone with him?

HEDDA: Some of the time.

BRACK: Did you leave the room at any time while he was here?

HEDDA: No.

BRACK: Try to remember. Were you out of the room—even for a moment?

HEDDA: Perhaps, yes, just for a moment. I was in the hallway.

BRACK: And where was your pistol case during that time?

HEDDA: It was locked up—in the—

BRACK: Well, where, Mrs. Tesman?

HEDDA: The case was on the writing table.

BRACK: Have you looked at it since then—to see whether both pistols are there?

HEDDA: No. I haven't.

BRACK: Well, there is no need. I saw the pistol that was found in Løvborg's pocket. I recognized it at once. I had seen it yesterday afternoon—and on other previous occasions.

HEDDA: Do you have it with you?

BRACK: No. The police have it.

HEDDA: And what will they do?

BRACK: They will try to find the owner.

HEDDA: And do you think they will succeed?

BRACK: *(bending over her and whispering)* No, Hedda Gabler—not so long as I say nothing.

HEDDA: *(looks at him, frightened)* And if you do say nothing—what then?

BRACK: *(shrugs his shoulders)* There is always the possibility that the pistol was stolen.

HEDDA: *(strongly)* Death rather than that.

BRACK: *(smiling)* Words, Mrs. Tesman, mere words. People don't do things like that.

HEDDA: *(ignoring him)* What if the pistol was not stolen? And what if the owner were discovered? What then?

BRACK: Well, Hedda, then there is the scandal.

HEDDA: The scandal!

BRACK: Yes. The scandal which frightens you to death. You see, you would be brought before the court. You and Mademoiselle Diana. She would have to explain what happened—whether the death was accidental or whether it was murder. Did the pistol go off as he was trying to take it out of his pocket, let us say, to threaten her? Or did she tear it out of his hand, shoot him, and then carefully replace it in his pocket? That would not be impossible—she is, I gather, quite capable of looking after herself.

HEDDA: The whole thing is unspeakably sordid. But it has nothing to do with *me*!

BRACK: No. But you would have to answer the question—why did you give the pistol to Eilert Løvborg? And when that fact is revealed, what conclusions will people draw? What will they think?

HEDDA: That thought had not entered my mind. *(bows her head)*

BRACK: Fortunately, there is no danger of that happening—so long as I say nothing.

HEDDA: *(looking up at him)* So, Judge Brack, I am in your power after all. From now on, I am at your disposal.

BRACK: *(whispers softly)* Dearest Hedda—believe me, I shall not take the slightest advantage of—

HEDDA: Nevertheless, I am in your power. I am subject to your will, your whim. I am a mere slave, a slave. *(rises quickly)* No. No. That is a thought that I cannot bear. Never.

BRACK: *(half-mocking look)* People usually get used to the inevitable.

HEDDA: *(looking at him)* Perhaps. *(Goes to writing table. Suppresses an involuntary smile. Imitates Tes-*

man's vocal mannerisms.) Well? Getting on, Jørgen, hmm?

TESMAN: Heaven knows. In any case, there's months of work here.

HEDDA: Just think. *(runs her hands through Mrs. Elvsted's hair)* Doesn't it seem strange to you, Thea? To be sitting here with Tesman, I mean—just as you must have sat with Eilert Løvborg.

MRS. ELVSTED: If only I could inspire your husband now—as I did then.

HEDDA: Oh, that will come—in time.

TESMAN: Yes, do you know, Hedda, I can almost feel something of the sort. Yes. But—won't you go and sit with Brack for a while?

HEDDA: Is there nothing I can do to help?

TESMAN: No, nothing. Not a thing. I trust you to keep Hedda company, my dear Brack.

BRACK: *(with a glance at her)* With the very greatest of pleasure.

HEDDA: Thank you. But I'm feeling rather tired this evening. I will go in and lie down on the sofa for a while.

TESMAN: Yes, do, my dear, hmm?

(Hedda leaves. Closes curtains. After a pause she is heard playing a dance on the piano.)

MRS. ELVSTED: *(getting up)* Oh, what is that?

TESMAN: *(runs to doorway)* Hedda, my dearest— please, no music. Not of that kind. Not tonight. Think of Aunt Rina. And of Eilert, too.

HEDDA: *(puts her head out between curtains)* And of

Aunt Julie. And of everyone else. After this I shall be quiet.

TESMAN: It's really not good for her to see us at work like this. I'll tell you what, Mrs. Elvsted. There's an empty room at Aunt Julie's. You can take it. And I will come over in the evenings and we can work there.

HEDDA: *(still in the other room)* I can hear what you're saying, Tesman. And how am I going to get through the evenings, here in this house?

TESMAN: Oh, I'm sure Judge Brack will be kind enough to drop in occasionally—even though I shall be out.

BRACK: *(in chair, calls out happily)* Oh, every evening, Mrs. Tesman, every evening. And with the greatest of pleasure. We two will get on wonderfully together.

HEDDA: *(in clear voice)* Yes, I'm sure you flatter yourself that we will, Judge Brack. Now that you are the one cock of the walk.

(A shot. The three rise to their feet.)

TESMAN: Oh, my God—what is she—

(Runs in, opens curtains. Mrs. Elvsted follows. Screams, confusion. Berte enters through the dining room door.)

TESMAN: Shot herself! In the temple!

BRACK: God—people—people don't do things like that.